MEN OF VIOLENCE

OTHER FIVE STAR WESTERN TITLES BY BILL BROOKS:

The Messenger (2009)

Blood Storm: A John Henry Cole Story (2012)

Frontier Justice: A John Henry Cole Story (2012)

Winter Kill: A John Henry Cole Story (2013)

Ride the Man Down: A John Henry Cole Story (2013)

A JOHN HENRY COLE STORY

MEN OF VIOLENCE

BILL BROOKS

FIVE STAR
A part of Gale, Cengage Learning

GALE
CENGAGE Learning·

Farmington Hills, Mich • San Francisco • New York • Waterville, Maine
Meriden, Conn • Mason, Ohio • Chicago

GALE
CENGAGE Learning·

LIBRARY OF CONGRESS CATALOGING-IN-PUBLICATION DATA

Brooks, Bill, 1943–
    Men of violence : a John Henry Cole story / by Bill Brooks.
        pages cm
    ISBN-13: 978-1-4328-2767-0 (hardcover)
    ISBN-10: 1-4328-2767-7 (hardcover)
    1. Private investigators—Fiction. I. Title.
PS3552.R65863M46 2014
813'.54—dc23   2013050377

First Edition. First Printing: May 2014.
Published in conjunction with Golden West Literary Agency.
Find us on Facebook– https://www.facebook.com/FiveStarCengage
Visit our website– http://www.gale.cengage.com/fivestar/
Contact Five Star™ Publishing at FiveStar@cengage.com

Printed in the United States of America
1 2 3 4 5 6 7 18 17 16 15 14

I want to see men with rough voices here.
Those who tame horses and train rivers;
Men whose bones ring out, who sing
With mouths full of sun and flint.

Federico García Lorca

CHAPTER ONE

The short man said—"They're in there."—and pointed to one of two dark cabins.

"Which one?" John Henry Cole asked.

"The one on the right, the other's my place."

"You're sure?" Cole asked.

"Sure I'm sure. They come to my place earlier and said they'd pay me to put them up, pay my woman to cook for them. That's their nags there in my corral. Still got the saddles on them because they are hurrying men. Come in looking all rough and dirty, like they'd been running from something for a long time."

Half a dozen saddle horses stood inside the corral.

"So how come you to turn them in if they're paying you?" Cole asked.

"They's reward money on them, I'm guessing, ain't they? Marshal can't come this far out of town. I heard about you, Cole. I heard you run thet detective agency, thet you was hell on wheels when it came to capturing men. Thet's why I got you."

"Yes, there's reward money on them," Cole said.

"That's what I figgered. Them ten dollars they paid me to put them up and have my woman cook for them ain't nothing compared to what the reward money must be. How much is it, anyways?"

John Henry Cole ignored the short man's query. He was a cautious man by nature, made more so by profession. Lawmen and ex-lawmen who were not cautious didn't last long on the frontier. "How come there's no light on in your house?" Cole said.

"No need of a light. Ain't nobody in there."

"You said a woman . . . that you had a woman who cooked for them."

"I took her to her sister's on my way to get you-all," the short man said. "I seen the way some of them was watching her . . . like dogs after a ham bone. Couldn't hardly trust to keep her around men like that. You know they probably done depredations all over the territory. They had them starved eyes."

John Henry Cole looked to his companions—other ex-lawmen, men like himself, men he knew and trusted, most of whom he'd worked with at one time or another, and now who worked for him: Lee Rivers, Ben Bradshaw, Fred Noon, Charley Hood. All good and true men.

Ever since his long ago days as a detective for Ike Kelly, Cole had always wanted to form his own detective agency, be the boss, the *jefe*. There wasn't that much work to be had as far as clients hiring him, but there were plenty of outlaws with rewards on their heads. He hoped to set aside a nice stake for his old age—if he lived to old age—and settle on that piece of land he'd bought himself a full two-day ride from Red Pony, across the border in southeastern Colorado. Pretty little piece of land with lots of good grass, and water running through it. He'd knocked together a good little house, too. He planned on ending up there, once he quit the game, and maybe raise some blooded horses. He liked horses better than he liked most humans.

The sort of humans he had to deal with in his chosen occupation were the rough trade—killers and rapists and thieves of every stripe. It had been that way most of his working life. He'd been a lawman since coming out alive of that great clash between the states. Had fought in it in such places as Rich

Mountain and Dry Woods Creek, New Bern, Shiloh, Savage's Station, and so many more he couldn't even remember. Blood killing, marching, fields of slaughter—it all became the same after a time. Nobody had been sorry to see it end—especially the boys who were still alive. Glad were they to go home with a gun and maybe a mule with U.S. branded on its flank. Glad were they to be relieved of the sharp scream of cannonball, the whine of Minié balls, the pleading cry of mortally wounded brethren. And even though the peace and silence were disturbing at first, eventually the nightmares concluded and life became normal again.

Being a soldier had taught John Henry Cole—as it did so many others—one employable skill: how to do gun work. And life as a soldier had hardened him, had inured him to hardship, long days and nights camped in the cold and rain, the ice and stolid summer heat. The Army had made him a sniper for a time because he was a very accurate shot, according to his commanding officer, who had ordered him to "go forth and commit slaughter and mayhem upon thine enemy." Killing from long distance or from a hidden place had seemed to Cole an unusually cruel form of warfare and he only did it one time. He threatened to walk away if they ever made him do it again, and they never did.

What John Henry Cole had learned was that there was always work for anyone who wanted to be a lawman and he banged around for ten years, working cattle towns in Kansas and New Mexico, rough spots like Las Vegas before he became a deputy United States marshal in the Western District Court in Fort Smith. The year he joined a new judge had been appointed—Judge Isaac Parker.

Such work required of a deputy to cross the Arkansas River via ferryboat and go into Indian Territory in search of killers, rapists, whiskey-runners who sold to the Indians, and other miscreants. He was often gone for weeks at a time in that country, rounding up the rounders, as they were called, before returning with a prison wagon full of the wanted who would stand trial before the judge. Some got sent off to prison and some to the house of correction in Detroit, Michigan, and some met their end by way of the hangman, George Maledon, a smallish man who never smiled. Of course such work as his relieved him, Cole had opined, of any humor he might have—the bang of the trap door sprung was as loud as a pistol shot.

Being a deputy was tough work, and had its surprises, too. Cole had once been shot by an Indian's woman, and that was a hell of a surprise. Where she'd shot him still aggravated him certain times of the year—mostly when the weather turned miserably cold.

He did that work for three years before he joined an old friend, Ike Kelly, in Cheyenne, Wyoming and became one of Kelly's detectives. He had really liked that sort of work and found it not only more interesting and perhaps a bit more dignified than being a deputy marshal, but it also paid better. But that was before Ike Kelly was murdered and death and mayhem had become intolerable. But maybe now that Cole had established his own agency it would be different. His agency was located in just about the worst, most dangerous place a man of good bearing could find—in Red Pony, in the Cherokee Strip, No Man's Land. It's where killers and bank robbers fled, into that narrow piece of land. It lay just across the border from Kansas and the west end of it butted up against Colorado and New Mexico, and south was Texas. They came from all over to take refuge in the Strip. So Cole had figured what better place to hunt outlaws for the money on their heads? In effect, the agency consisted of men who were bounty hunters, but also of men who were honorable.

Cole believed that every man deserved a fair trial, even the worst of them. Not all bounty hunters held such a sense of justice. Rewards often stated dead or alive, and a lot of bounty hunters preferred bringing in their quarry dead rather than alive. Of course, it was personally safer that way. And though neither John Henry Cole nor any of the men he had recruited were murderers, every last one of them had shot and killed men at one time or another. You had to have grit to do the dirty business of capturing outlaws. And life wasn't always kind or fair; a few of the men Cole *would* have liked to have recruited had themselves been killed and buried by the men they'd pursued.

A woman Cole had once been in love with—although there had been several in his past—had called him and others like him "men of violence." He could not disagree with her.

"Are you ever troubled by bad dreams?" she'd asked.

"No," he had said.

"I find that strange," she had said.

"I think you only have bad dreams if you feel guilty about something," he had replied.

"But killing a man is a thing to feel guilty about, isn't it?"

"Not always. Not if he's about to take your life or the life of another, or if he's taken lives and needs to be stopped, and there is only one way he'll let himself be stopped."

"Sometimes I wonder if you're without a soul, John Henry."

"Sometimes I wonder the same thing."

She had ended up marrying a banker and moving to Wisconsin where he heard she died one long winter of the Spanish flu. He felt badly for a long time because he had loved her, and she him. But sometimes, he told himself, love alone isn't enough. He decided he'd stop drinking, that the whiskey was distorting his wisdom. He'd often heard his mama's warning about how liquor is the thief of men's brains. He figured a man getting as long in the tooth as he ought to buckle down and save up for his retiring years. He figured to move to that piece of ground and that cabin in Colorado when the day came that he knew he was finished with any business that had to do with gun work.

Now, as midnight neared, he stood along with the others, there in the short man's orchard, watching the darkened dwelling where presumably the Sam Starr gang had taken refuge. Cole hoped it wouldn't turn bloody, that the men inside would have enough sense to know they were surrounded when he gave the warning to them. Sometimes the worst and hardest criminals gave up the easiest. And Sam Starr was about the worst there was.

"We'll leave the horses here," Cole said to the others. Then to the short man who'd summoned them: "You wait with the horses."

"You'll get no argument from me," the short man said, and seemed eager to co-operate. "I'm just a poor peach farmer, I ain't no fighter."

Cole and the others pulled the Winchesters from their saddle scabbards and advanced slowly through the orchard.

A full moon had cast its spell upon the land and shone so brightly it was like the dream of a day. The five detectives moved like shadows, keeping close to the fruit trees that had long since borne their bounty and now stood as barren as Biblical women.

The night air was biting, but most had dressed for the cold, wearing heavy Mackinaws and kidskin gloves and one, Charley Hood, a scarf his wife had knitted him, wrapped around his neck.

To the right of the refuge cabin, some dozen or so yards, was a tool shed. Between the two cabins and slightly to the rear stood a privy. The corral, with the sleeping saddle horses standing, was several feet to the west of the short man's cabin. There was about thirty or so feet of open ground between orchard and the two dwellings.

"If we can make it across this open space without being spotted," Cole said in a low voice, "we can surround that shack and order them out. There can't be any escape."

The others nodded in agreement.

They studied the shack for a moment longer, then advanced on cat's feet, keeping low, Winchesters gripped in hands, each with a shell already jacked in the chamber, and each with at least one and mostly two loaded pistols.

These were seasoned men, men who knew that when you went into a fight you'd best go in with a lot of firepower. And the men who they hunted knew the same thing. A man with just a single six-shooter was asking for it in a fight.

With hand signals, John Henry Cole motioned for the men to take up position—signaling Lee Rivers and Ben Bradshaw to swing around to the left of the cabin, and Fred Noon and Charley Hood to the right, knowing that one would take up a position near the front and the other would split around to the back. Cole positioned himself directly in line with the front door.

They knew, because they'd planned it, that once in position Cole would give the order for the men inside to come out with their hands in the air, giving them every chance to surrender peacefully. If that failed initially, they would fire several rounds from all sides into the shack just to let those inside know that they were in fact surrounded and stood no chance.

If worse came to worst, there would be a hell of a gun battle and somebody was bound to get killed. Cole hoped that it would not come to that.

He waited, kneeled on the cold ground, his breath coming in small white puffs of frosty air, his mind oddly calm as it almost always was on the verge of battle, knowing that the others were the same way—calm, efficient professionals, that once you've cheated death, as every one of them had, some more than once, there wasn't much more to fear. They called it "seeing the angels."

He counted off the time in his head to allow the others to get in position. When he figured they were ready, he picked up a fist-size rock and pitched it against the cabin's door, then called: "You inside the cabin, come out with your hands up, you are surrounded by an armed posse!"

His words cut through the night's stillness and seemed to drift all the way to the moon that now stood high up in the sky, looking down like a curious eye.

When no immediate response came, Cole pointed his rifle skyward and pulled the trigger, and the bang it made cracked through the coldness like the earth had suddenly split open.

That's when those in the privy and those in the tool shed and those inside the short man's cabin opened fire on those who'd surrounded the building and caught the detectives in a withering crossfire. Suddenly the hunters had become the hunted.

Cole knew almost before the first bullet clipped him that he had been duped into an ambush—that the short man wasn't at all what he'd passed himself off as, an innocent orchard-keeper trying to get rich from reward money. Suddenly they were at war—a war of survival. Cole could not know how many guns there were firing at them, but a lot and from everywhere. The flash of gunfire sparkled in the moon-struck light.

Cole turned to fire at the building that was nearest to him. He heard someone scream, but it was from the other side of the shack where he'd sent his men. Cole fired as fast as he could lever his rifle, but then another bullet punched him between shoulder bone and collar bone and knocked him down. His entire left arm went instantly numb and he lost his grip on his rifle.

He jerked one of his two pistols from its holster with his good hand and cocked and fired, cocked and fired, and he was hit for the third time, this time in the side, just below his ribs, and it took a piece of his meat with it.

He was in the killing zone. He knew, if he couldn't escape it quickly, he would be a dead man. Cole managed to rise and, while still cocking and pulling the trigger on his Remington, headed for the orchard, even though he couldn't be sure that the short man wasn't there, waiting to clean up on any who came back for their horses. But if he was, Cole intended to kill him for being a Judas to them all.

Bullets clipped Cole's heels and he thought he'd been shot in the foot. He stumbled and fell face down, but twisted around to see that it was only the heel of his boot that had been shot off. He fired his last bullet at the cabin, then reached for his other pistol as he gained his feet once more and went in search of the short man and the horses.

But the short man and the horses were gone. The orchard was empty of all but the barren-women trees, their gnarled black arms reaching, dark and twisted, against the moonlight.

Cole felt the hot seep of his blood turn cold, like ice water, as it ran down his chest and side and soaked his shirt and trousers. The racket of gunfire continued, then abated after several more minutes.

Cole was down to a single pistol for firepower and the flame of pain was starting to burn him up. He gritted his teeth as he worked his way through the orchard, trying to circle around the buildings to get to the other side, to reach his men, to take up the fight with them, and wipe out the bastards ambushing them. All thoughts of justice and fair trials were set aside now. It was a matter of sheer survival—not his choice but theirs.

When he reached the westerly edge of the orchard, he could see the back of the cabin where much of the gunfire had come from. He saw no rear door to it, not even a window. He limped along, keeping low, Remington in hand, cocked and ready to fire.

Everything was silent now, quiet as a graveyard, and this in itself was disturbing because Cole knew that if his men were still alive, they'd still be fighting. But they surely couldn't all be dead, could they?

A creek twisted through the rear part of the property and meandered back again toward the other buildings before it snaked on to the north, and Cole waded along in it to keep low cover of the cabin and any of the other places an assassin might be stationed. The creek water was bitterly cold and filled his boots, and when he reached the right spot, he crawled out of it, lying flat to the ground to make himself less of a target.

His breath came in short, hard gasps as the pain from his wounds seared into his brain like a hot iron. Then suddenly the night air exploded with stampeding horses, and John Henry Cole rose halfway up in time to see riders bursting from the corral, their mounts knocking down the rails as they rode off, whooping and firing their pistols into the moonlight. And just like that, they had escaped.

In a way it was almost a blessing they had ridden off instead of staying to fight, for Cole suspected that whoever among his men was yet alive was probably as wounded as he was and not in much condition to withstand a gang of armed and vicious killers who would show them none of the mercy they might have been given if captured.

He struggled to his feet slowly, painfully, and then staggered forth, calling out to the others—Charley, Ben, Lee, and Fred.

Only one answered—Charley Hood, the one who wore the scarf his wife had knitted, as much for luck, she'd said when she gave it to him, as for warmth. In the moonlight Cole saw the bodies of his detectives, lying still, except for Charley, who sat upright, his legs stretched out in front of him—as if he had simply lain down and gone to sleep.

Cole needed no doctor to tell him that other than Charley the rest were dead, and cursed whatever god would allow such a thing to happen, who would allow such good men to be slain by such evil ones.

CHAPTER TWO

Together, leaning on each other, John Henry Cole and Charley Hood limped to the cabin where, inside, they found the body of an old gray-haired man stretched out and face down, stiff as a board, lying in a strip of moonlight that angled in through the one and only window.

Cole struck a match, found an oil lamp, and lit it. Then he took a bed sheet from what was the old man's bed and tore it into strips and bound Charley's wounds. He had been shot through the right thigh and left calf, the same bullet apparently piercing both legs. Then Charley did his nursing of Cole in turn, holding the lamp's light close to the wounds in Cole's side and shoulder, and packing them with strips from the sheet.

"Them bullets went clean through, both of them," Charley said.

"We were lucky, I guess," Cole said. Then, walking slightly off kilter, he went to the window. Looking out, he could still see Fred Noon's body lying on its side a dozen yards away, just like he'd laid down and taken a nap.

"Damn it to hell," Cole said, and slumped down.

"This was that old man's place and not that short fellow's," Charley said, looking at the corpse of the old man. Cole took out his makings and fashioned two cigarettes, and handed one to Charley, then struck a match and held the flame to the ends of their cigarettes.

"They bamboozled us, John Henry."

18

"We got took like schoolboys offered candy," Cole said. "I should have questioned that little bastard a lot harder than I did."

"Don't beat yourself up," Charley said, drawing on his smoke, then exhaling through his nostrils. "None of us had any doubts about that fellow's story."

"The reward money clouded my judgment," Cole confessed.

"I feel real bad for Fred and Ben and Lee, is all," Charley said. "Feel bad for their wives. And Lee's got a brand new little one, too."

"I know it."

Cole cradled his Winchester as he smoked. Somehow smoking seemed to help ease the pain some.

"They got our damn' horses and everything," Cole said after moments of reflection, prompted by the need to talk, to explain it.

"Then you're going to have to go for help, because I don't think I could walk a mile with my shot-up legs," Charley said.

"You think with my help you can make it to the road until somebody comes along?"

"Yeah, if I don't bleed out first."

"Hell, you've had worse happen to you," Cole said. "That time in Tahlequah, you remember, when that woman shot you and nearly blew off your nuts?"

"Christ, don't remind me. Those Tahlequah women are real hardcases."

"You were trying to arrest her man," Cole said. "She didn't take kindly to it."

"He got clean away, and me lying there, bleeding like a stuck pig. I should have stuck to barbering. That's what I was doing when you wired me to come and join you-all in this venture. I got out of the life once, and I should have stayed out of it."

"Yeah, but you'd have died of boredom, cutting men's hair

all day, chewing the fat. Men like us weren't made to fit our hands to no kind of work but this."

"Would have at least died in my own damned bed and not in some shack that has a dead man in it," Charley moaned.

"Let's try and get some sleep."

"Way my legs hurt, I doubt I can sleep."

"Well, we ought to try and wait here till daylight, start out first thing in the morning, get up on the road, and maybe somebody will come along and take us back to Red Pony."

"Red Pony," Charley grunted, like it was a thing he was trying to spit out.

They smoked until their shucks burned down and stubbed them out, and then sat, trying to fall into some semblance of sleep as the lamp's wick burned out and the moon's light gave up and faded with the earth's turning until the palest gray light of dawn came.

Cole opened his eyes, having half forgotten that he'd been shot, and went to stand up, but it felt, when he tried, like something had nailed him to the wall. It took every ounce of his strength and grit to get to his feet.

Charley had slumped over and was snoring slightly, his hat crushed under his head, his bandages seeping blood from his wounds.

"Charley, it's morning, get up."

Cole had to shake him until Charley's eyes fluttered open.

"*Waugh . . . !*"

"It's morning. We got to see if we can make it up to the road."

Charley struggled to stand, using his Winchester like a cane.

"Put your arm over my shoulders," Cole said.

They went out and did not look toward the place where their friends and partners lay, their bloody clothes frosted over from the cold night, even their hair, and moved toward the road they knew ran south of the peach orchard and then roughly west, the way they'd first come to the place.

It took them the better part of an hour to make it to the road, having to stop every few feet so Charley could catch the breath that the pain in his legs was stealing from him.

"Maybe you best go on without me and get some help, John Henry."

"No, I'll not leave you behind."

Finally they made it up to the road after fording a ditch full of cockleburs that snagged their clothes, and rested alongside it, waiting, hoping for someone to come along.

Cole checked his pocket watch quite often, eager to get help for Charley, eager to get himself patched up and after that gang of assassins. At least that's what he told himself.

The morning wind blew, sharp and cold, and added to their miseries, but the coldness helped stanch the blood, and for that they knew that they should be grateful.

Charley made them shucks this time, but had a hard time lighting them, his hands shaking so, whether from cold or pain. Cole took the matches and held a flame for each of them.

"I sure could use a stiff one right about now," Charley said.

"We get back to Red Pony, I'll buy you all you want."

"You quit, didn't you?"

"Yes, had to."

"Why'd you have to?"

"I knew where it was taking me."

"There's worse things can happen to a man than being a drunk," Charley said.

"Maybe so," Cole said, remembering why he'd finally quit. A medico over in Fort Smith had told him that some had an unusual weakness for liquor and those that did couldn't touch a drop lest they fall into an ocean of it. Cole had figured from past experience that he was just such a man.

For a time he'd drifted far and wide, and reached a point

where his life was no good, where he'd become worse than a tramp or a bum, living hand to mouth and all the time shivering so badly he couldn't do nothing but shake like a bad-wheeled wagon. His clothes were soiled and his body stinking, his hair a tangled mess, his face gone unshaven. Liquor seemed not only to steal his mind but also his pride. He thought back then to those days that he'd drunk to forget the life he'd lived, and also the one he hadn't. Early on he'd lost a wife and infant son to the milk sickness, this, after returning home from a war that had taken its toll in ways he could not measure, nor admit to.

Then, later, he'd met a Cherokee woman, Anna Rain, up in the Nations while he'd been working as a United States deputy marshal, and again fell in love. The problem was her father had disapproved of him. So he'd left, wandering some more. When he saw Anna again in the Nations, she was married. He also learned that they'd had a son who had turned into a young outlaw. Thomas. Although he'd rescued the boy and had returned him to Anna, he hadn't seen either of them in several years, though he did think of them often enough. He'd promised to return one day and settle down, but when he'd gone back there, they were gone from that country. Some who claimed to have known them said they'd gone up to Canada to avoid the lawdogs that were after the boy. Thomas had remained a wanted man for his previous criminal activities. Cole had let him go instead of taking him to Fort Smith to stand trial. Thomas was a good kid who'd just got mixed up with the wrong company. Cole never did find them again. And so he drank worse even than before to kill the memory.

When Cole had hit rock bottom, there was only one way to go—to kill himself or get sober. One was easy, the other hard. He took the hard way. But, by God, if he had a bottle setting right there next to him right then, he was damned if he wouldn't take a drink. What was asked of him by himself didn't any longer seem to tote.

"They shot us to pieces, Charley," Cole said idly.

"Hell, John Henry, you're not telling me nothing I don't already know."

The sun finally broke through the glaucous sky and shattered upon the earth in bright, stabbing rays that gave the illusion of warmth, but there was no warmth to it, certainly for such shot-up men, shivering in their pain and desolation.

Then back through the place from which they'd struggled they heard the yip and snarl of coyotes, and Cole swore, and stood and aimed his pistol with his good but blood-crusted hand, and fired every round in his chambers toward the sounds until they quit yipping and snarling.

Neither Cole nor Charley had to say what it was. They both knew what it was the coyotes had come for.

"Those sons-of-bitches," Cole said, doing his best to reload but dropping bullets as he tried.

"Here, give your guns to me," Charley said. "I got shot-up legs, but my hands are good." He took Cole's pistols and reloaded them for him, and handed them back one by one.

Cole started to cross back over the ditch, in order to return, but Charley said: "It won't do no good. They'll just come back no matter how many of them you might shoot. They are creatures who don't know no difference to eat a kilt deer or a shot man. They're just the same thing is all. We can't bury our boys, and we can't tote them, and if we go back and stand guard over them, we'll be joining them."

Cole looked grim, staring back toward the orchard that lay so far in the distance he couldn't even see it, or the cabin and other buildings.

"We'll get them boys out of there," Charley said. "Sooner or later, we'll get them and bury them proper."

With the sun straight up, the sound of a wagon came down

the road, the bray of mules, and the voice of a man singing a church hymn:

> *Tho' like the wanderer,*
> *The sun goes down,*
> *Darkness be over me,*
> *My rest a stone;*
> *Yet in my dreams I'd be*
> *Nearer, my God, to Thee,*
> *Nearer, my God, to Thee. . . .*

"God damn," Charley said. "Praise Jesus and whoever that fellow is a-coming."

CHAPTER THREE

Preacher Man drove the wagon. It was pulled by a matched pair of Missouri mules, one jack and one jenny, guiding them with sure hands. He was nearly as black as the broadcloth suit he wore, though the trousers were shiny in the knees and rump. His head was covered by a pancake hat, cocked slightly at an angle. And though he wore brogans of rough brown leather, his feet were protected by silk stockings purchased for him by a Memphis whore, his beloved at the time, a girl known by the denizens as Juicy Lou, she of golden curls and eyes as blue as any Kansas sky on a summer's day.

Preacher Man had figured to change her with both the lamb's blood of his sweet Lord and greater passion than she'd ever known, but changed she would not be, for she liked the sporting life more than Preacher Man and all his angels and all his fancy Bible talk and promises of pearly gates, and refused to go away with him on his journey into the "Great American West" as he termed it, to "bring salvation to the savages and forlorn, the miscreants, the down-trodden, and the sinful." He declaimed that the Lord had called him to venture forth across the Mississippi and take the message all the way to the far blue ocean. He'd said her company would bring him much succor and delight.

"The hell you say," she had replied.

She may just as well have taken a hammer and bruised his heart with it. He had begged and pleaded, but she would not budge from her billet above the boulevard where men came for the specific reason of carousing. She, like all the other soiled doves, would stand upon her balcony, waving a white silk hanky to attract the strollers and idlers, then when she caught their attention, she would flash her supple bosoms that were to Preacher Man like fresh pomegranates ripe for the plucking. In fact, this was the very way in which they had met, Juicy Lou and he, as he'd come into the French Quarter seeking sinners to convert, and maybe imbibe just a bit, for a man whose voice rings loud and often tends to go dry after a time and is in need of lubrication. Even the Lord knew the healing need of wine and had turned water into it on certain occasions. Why, then, would the Savior hold it against a man to slake his thirst after pronouncing the Good Word to those most in need of it? Preacher Man had reasoned.

And didn't Jesus himself consort with such as tax collectors and prostitutes, hadn't he gone down among them, the worst of the worst? But even Preacher Man had to admit to himself that the good Lord probably never met anyone quite so comely or enticing as Juicy Lou. It was as if she'd cast a spell over him that blinded his mind and good sense and he had ended up falling hard in love with Lou, but, alas, she not so much with Preacher Man.

And so he'd left that place, that den of iniquity, with a renewed sense of what his mission was about, with a shame that stained his soul like scarlet wine spilled on a fine Persian rug, and set off for the West, traveling its byways and pikes, stopping in towns and burgs and villages of every stripe and preaching to whoever would hear him. He laid hands upon the lame and blind and deaf, like the Lord himself had, and caused them to walk and see and hear again—at least until he cleared town with a pocketful of donations.

Once a posse of locals had caught up with him and demanded

his surrender as a fake and impostor.

"I demand to know how you can say such things," he had argued.

And when the posse men tried to answer, to suggest he'd somehow hypnotized or cast a spell over the poor souls he'd claimed to have healed, he said simply: "Ye of little faith. Am I to be my brother's keeper?" And many other such sage witticisms, so many in fact that he had confounded them with his logic and Bible quoting. They had no answers to what was true, what he'd pointed out in the very passages of the gospels, and had showed them. "Did not even Jesus's own mother and disciples doubt?" he had concluded.

And when a few still looked skeptical, he had said, waving the Good Book in their faces: "Do you believe that this is the infallible word of God, or do you admit to being an atheist?"

They had all nodded their heads that they indeed *did* believe even though he knew some of them probably did not, but they would never admit it in front of their companions. For what man wants to be known as *godless*?

"Well then, what more is there to discuss?" he had argued, and turned them back, and on he went up that road and many others like it. And now here he had come around the bend of his latest road and saw there on the edge of it two men who were bloody and bandaged, who looked blanched and in pain and in need of salvation of one sort or another. He hauled back on the reins of the mules much to the mules' dislike, for they had smelled water somewhere ahead and were thirsting to get to it.

"Whoa up, Mary and Joseph!"

John Henry Cole stood, helped Charley Hood to his feet, and said: "We're in need of a ride to town, but we're also in need of getting our friends as well. . . ."

Preacher Man looked about. "What friends?" he said. "I don't see nobody else."

"Back yonder," Cole said, jerking his thumb over his shoulder.

Preacher Man looked. All he saw was gnarled vegetation.

"How come they just didn't walk up here to the road with you-all?"

"Because they're dead," Charley growled, weary of all the questions.

Preacher Man got down and helped Cole put Charley in the wagon's bed, laid him next to the folded canvas tent and steamer trunk with its leather straps and brass fittings. Everything was crammed in the wagon a man would need to sustain himself on the road to salvation or anywhere else he chose to go—cooking pots, sacks of flour, sugar, coffee, salted ham, cans of beans, and potted meat, blankets, pillows, even a small box of Bibles that could be sold to converts.

"You got any whiskey, have you?" Charley said.

Preacher Man reached in under his seat and produced a crock jug.

"It's not wine, but it's close," he said.

"Well, then that's close enough for me," Charley said, and took a swallow, then another. He handed the jug to Cole and Cole reached for it and held it a moment, then handed it back to Preacher Man without partaking. He knew that one drink would lead to two, and then three, and it'd keep going until the jug was empty and he was still craving more.

"No," he said, "but thank you kindly."

Preacher Man helped Cole up to the wagon seat beside him and said: "Point the way, pilgrim."

Cole directed him around till they reached the orchard by going down a trace cut through the winter dried weeds and brown grass that crackled under the iron-rimmed wheels. The sun had warmed enough through the winter sky to melt off the night's layer of frost.

"Looks like you can get through there," Cole said, pointing, his fingers crusted in dried blood.

They reached the yard and the cabin, then Cole and Preacher Man climbed down and went first to one body—Fred Noon—and then the others, and it took all their effort to haul the corpses back to the wagon and get them in, and stacked like cord wood, their limbs stiffened in death. The coyotes thankfully hadn't done a lot of damage. Preacher Man covered them with some of the canvas from his preaching tent, much to everyone's relief. For to look upon the dead faces of pals was grief itself.

The wagon springs groaned under the load but the mules were big and stout and used to pulling heavy loads. Preacher Man had bought them off a farmer gone bust—a neighbor of the notorious James boys, who had yet to be caught, although they and their gang of cousins, the Youngers, had been shot to rags recently some place up in Minnesota.

So off they headed to Red Pony, a dozen miles distant, but a ride that seemed endless to John Henry Cole and Charley Hood, who, while eager to return to what they deemed a safe haven, were wont not to return at all for the bad news they'd have to deliver to the kin and friends of the dead men.

To return home again as the defeated was more onerous than one might imagine, and it was to these two men of honor and courage as it would have been to any defeated army. But still they went.

Chapter Four

Dr. Genius Fish had been a surgeon during the War Between the States. He had patched and amputated and nursed all sorts of boys shot full of holes, lanced with bayonets, pierced with shrapnel, sick with the diseases of dysentery, scurvy, rickets, and the pox they would catch from local whores in such places as New Orleans and Nashville. All creatures great and small, he considered them, boys mostly, from the farms of Ohio and Indiana and Michigan. It had seemed like the boys from Massachusetts and New York and the like were a bit more sophisticated, but not by much when it came to catching the pox.

He'd become something of an expert on treating gunshot wounds and figured he could make a fair living after the war was over by going first to Arkansas and later to Indian Territory. Doc Fish was a restless spirit who wanted to see what the West was truly like and not simply from the renderings of painters and photographers. It was his sense of adventure, along with patriotism, that got him into the war, although it had cost him a lot more than he could have anticipated—sleep being his greatest bedevilment, and human suffering not far behind. He had cut off enough young arms and legs, stared into enough fearful young eyes, and pretty soon whiskey came to be the only medicine that seemed worth a damn—both for the patient and the practitioner.

So, yes, he had become a boozer, but he no longer cared much. He'd much rather hang out with the boys down at one of the local saloons, listening to them telling ribald stories, than sit in any posh male club or society, listening to all the stuffy pontifications of men whose greatest decision of the day was what to have for supper. He liked the West and he liked the men of the West, the cowpunchers and teamsters and gamblers and pimps. He liked the women, too—those salty harlots and their ilk. The West was a place where a man could be who he wanted to be, could reinvent himself a dozen times over if he wanted to. It was often a place of danger, but a place of great beauty as well. And even the beauty could kill you if you became too enamored of it. There was no more rough-and-tumble place than the Cherokee Strip and he liked it right down to its red dirt.

Impoverished men came and got rich, and rich men came and ended up impoverished. Whores married cattle barons and chaste women married cowboys, and so it went. And you never did know when gunfire might break out and a dead man be found on the streets come morning. There was for Doc Fish a certain euphoria that came with the unexpected.

Doc had a paramour, too—he nearly always had, whatever town he hit, and pretty quickly, because he understood the powers of a woman were like an anesthetic to a broken heart, a suitable elixir for loneliness. He was with his inamorata that midday morning when Preacher Man came hauling into town with two wounded men and three dead ones. He'd been getting dressed in Louisa's room when he heard the rattling of the wagon, the bray of the mules. The window was slightly open in spite of the cold weather because Doc believed it benefited a man's constitution to sleep always with open windows, winter and summer. He went and peered out Louisa's lace-curtained window and down upon the wide hard-packed street.

He recognized John Henry Cole and Charley Hood right off, for they were men of honor and not the rough-cut killers that often practiced the gun profession. They were businessmen, enterprising and not unlike himself. Sometimes they brought him shot-up men they'd tracked down, men that Cole and Charley had wounded in gunfights—brought them forth with compassion and had Doc mend them before turning them over to the law. John Henry Cole was a man that Doc could and did admire, as he did Charley and the others who were part of the bounty-hunter squad, though they preferred calling themselves detectives. In a sense, Doc thought, Cole and the others were not like those they hunted.

Doc saw by their bloody bandages they were wounded, saw, too, pairs of boots sticking out from under the tarp.

"Lord Almighty," he said to his lover who was still lounging about in a silk wrapper Doc had given her the previous Christmas.

"What is it, baby?" she wondered.

"Looks like John Henry and them ran into some bad trouble."

She came and looked over his shoulder. Louisa LaFontaine was the tallest woman in the entire Cherokee Outlet as far as anybody knew, well over six feet three inches, and as much hair as two women, a pretty russet color that looked like spun red threads. She was handsome in her own particular way with a longish broad face. She ran a bawdy house of girls called the Dove Cage, though she herself no longer practiced the profession.

"I humped my last cowpuncher years ago," she'd told Doc.

Doc was a smallish man and quite liked the fact that his inamorata was so tall. He'd said to her upon their first meeting: "Why you're as tall as the President."

"You mean was," she had said.

"Was," he had stood corrected, for the President by then was no more than a corpse entombed in Illinois.

"What do you think happened, Doc?" she asked now.

"Gun play," he said. "Fooling with guns is a lot like fooling with snakes . . . sooner or later you're going to get hurt." Doc put on his shirt and trousers, socks and shoes, coat and hat, and said dramatically: "We'll meet again, Kathleen."

"Louisa," she corrected.

"I know, sweet," he said with an impish smile, "but I don't know of any songs with Louisa in them."

He did not wait to hear her reply, if any at all. Louisa's one deficiency was her sense of humor; she had none.

Doc met the men in the street and shouted: "Take them to my office, follow me!"

Preacher Man drove his wagon behind the fast-stepping medico.

"I'll feel plum relieved," Charley said, "if ol' Doc don't kill me trying to patch me up."

Cole remained quite pensive, his thoughts on the dead beneath the canvas in the back of the wagon. His own wounds ached like rotted teeth, worse, but he stood the pain nonetheless because he didn't know any other way but to stand it.

Doc stepped up on the sidewalk in front of his office and a door that read in gold leaf lettering on the frosted windowpane: *Dr. Fish, M.D. & Surgeon.*

"Let me help you fellows in," he said after swinging the door wide.

By then a crowd of the curious had gathered, for men wrapped in bloody bandages and looking nearly as blanched white as fish bellies were a thing to be curious about. Everyone in Red Pony knew John Henry Cole and Charley Hood and about Cole's detective agency. Most thought it was a hell of a good idea in a place where there was too little law and too much country to cover. Where once vigilance committees had helped fill in the gap of scarce lawmen, now stood a group of professional ex-lawmen who knew their business of capturing killers and were not indiscriminate as were so many of the stock detectives often hired by cattle operations who sometimes killed the innocent right along with the guilty.

Men, women, and children came to bear witness to something they thought they'd never see—John Henry Cole and Charley Hood shot up and three of their brethren dead as stone. Gasps and huzzahs rippled through the gathered, the names of the dead whispered on lips: "Why it's Fred Noon, and that is Ben, poor ol' Ben . . . and look how badly Lee's been shot. My God!"

"Somebody go get Ben's missus. . . ."

"Will somebody let my wife know as well," Charley said, being helped off the back of the wagon, his legs now so aflame with pain that he could barely stand.

Both he and Cole were helped inside, and Charley was laid on Doc's cutting table, Cole on a tufted horsehair divan in the waiting room. Doc was giving orders to anyone who would listen and take heed: "Get me some hot water going on that stove, and Philpot, go in that cabinet and get me that bottle of alcohol and the one of chloroform."

"But I can't read Doc, which is which?"

"Oh, for Christ's sake! Go get Hester. She knows what to do."

Somebody went.

Hester Piccadilly was a homely woman but had a giving heart, kind and compassionate almost beyond belief. She'd do a favor or a good turn for anybody and never complain about being put out. She'd worked for Doc Fish ever since he had first hit town and advertised for a nursing assistant. She'd had no qualifications other than being a member of the Good Pilgrims Quaker United Holiness Church and having a deep and abiding compassion for humankind and animals, too.

Doc, being the ladies' man that he was, wasn't so sure about hiring a homely woman to work with him. But on the other hand, he was smart enough to know that if you mixed business and pleasure, you'd soon enough end up having neither, so in that regard Doc thought Hester to be perfect.

Hester'd never been married, but had once been deeply in love with a man a decade younger than she. He had been of youthful form and vigor and had gone off to fight in the war, his name Jim Hardcandy. She'd tried her best to talk him out of it for fear she'd never get a second chance at love, but he said he was bound for glory and wanted to kill his share of Billy Yanks, said it with the softest drawl she'd ever heard, a voice that was nearly feminine. Their parting kiss lasted nearly a minute, and then he was gone from her life, never to be seen again. She'd offered: "I'll give myself to you, Jim, if you wish. I am a virgin, but I will betroth my virginity if you'll promise to return and marry me."

He'd blushed red as a beet and admitted that he himself was also a virgin.

"Well, then," Hester had said, "we shall cast our die together and it will bind us together forever and ever. . . ."

They'd fumbled a bit getting their clothes off there in the darkened room of Hester's father's house—the father sick in bed with the gout. Just then he was out of earshot of the young people. "We must be somewhat quiet about it, Jim," Hester had cautioned, "so that Father does not hear and come limping in his nightclothes in the dark and find us. He'll beat you bloody with his cane."

Perhaps it was this warning that threw Jim off his feed, or the fact that he'd never before had sexual congress, but as it turned out their love was not consummated that night or any other, although not for lack of trying. Jim, over-eager, just couldn't contain his passion, and had groaned loudly as desire broke from him like a wave crashing upon a rock. Then Jim, embarrassed at what had happened, ran off to the war and was killed at Peach Tree Creek from a bayonet through the throat. Hester had read his name on the death lists posted at the courthouse and wept for days and vowed never to fall in love or marry— and no other man had ever asked her.

So she came running when one of the townsmen summoned her, saying how Doc needed her. It was all bloody rags and dark, oozing wounds, forceps and needles and silk threads for stitching.

"You boys are damn' lucky brutes," Doc opined, "for not one of you has a bullet lodged in his body, otherwise I'd have to knock you cold with ether and dig the lead out of you because of sepsis."

"Well, hell, Doc," Charley said, "glad you let me know how lucky I am. Now I can go and celebrate." After which he promptly passed out from the loss of blood while his wife waited in an anteroom for Doc to come and tell her how Charley was doing.

"He'll live, but he will probably be hobbling around a while," he said, much to her relief.

Doc fixed Cole a sling for his arm even though it wasn't broken, but where the bullet passed through between shoulder and breastbone, it had temporarily paralyzed some nerves so that he couldn't use the arm for a time.

The dead were taken to Stick Krebs, the undertaker. Krebs, like Doc, had been in the war, but as an embalmer's assistant and had had plenty of practice preparing the dead for burial, too many dead in his estimation. The only saving grace had been that the only boys who got embalmed were those whose families had paid, mostly in advance, for the embalming. The cost was $50 for officers and $25 for enlisted men, and sometimes there would be upward of a hundred poor wretches a day to have their veins pumped full of the arsenic-based embalming fluid, but beauties they'd be when he finished, almost as if they'd simply gone to sleep, those, at least, whose wounds were not horrific.

Yes, Krebs had become inured to the business of death and went about his work efficiently, often humming happy tunes while preparing the bodies of dead men and women, even children, murdered or otherwise, though the children still caused him to reach for the bottle of peach brandy he kept close at hand.

"Got three for you, Stick," one of the men who carried in the dead lawmen said. Stick was Krebs's nickname because of how thin he was, almost cadaverous, as if he were slowly metamorphosing into one of his clients.

"I asked you not to call me that, Hollister," Krebs said with a deep gravelly voice.

"Sure, sure, Stick, where you want them?"

He gazed upon the passive faces of each of them—Ben Bradshaw, Fred Noon, and Lee Rivers—men he'd known. On occasion he had gotten drunk with them, or played cards. How odd, he thought, to have seen two of them just yesterday morning at the Sunshine Café, eating breakfast and joking about something that caused them to laugh. And Fred, the sober one of the three, who rarely if ever laughed about anything, he was big and gruff with reddish walrus mustaches and a chest so thick it had seemed not even a bullet could pierce it. But a bullet *had* pierced it; in fact several had. There were three dark wounds found in the torso when Krebs cut away the bloody shirt, the flesh otherwise so white it almost looked like plaster.

Lee Rivers's wounds were more apparent—shot through face and back of the head. And Fred Noon was shot twice in the back with the bullets exploding out the front. Krebs surmised that if Fred had not been killed outright, he surely would have ended up paralyzed by the wound directly through the spine.

"Consider yourself lucky, my good fellow," he muttered.

Krebs got out his embalming equipment—copper tank, rubber tubes, long puncture needle—and set to work while humming "Gary Owen", glad that this time it was not children.

Word spread rapidly throughout the town about the shooting, the ambush by the Sam Starr gang on the detectives, and the attendant fears that the gang might hear that they hadn't wiped out Cole and his men completely, and so would come to Red Pony looking for them. What then?

Several of them sought out the town marshal, Lou Ford, and asked if a vigilance committee should be formed to try and track down the killers? But if the killers were canny enough to outfox and murder professional ex-lawmen the likes of John Henry Cole and Charley Hood, who among the local townsmen could stand up to them?

Lou Ford was a thoughtful man who weighed every decision thoroughly before acting and concluded that the best course of action—since the town was too small to have deputies, and knowing the general make-up of the men among them—was to send for the county sheriff, Birdy Peach.

"I'll go and send the wire to Sheriff Peach myself," Lou assured them. His word seemed good enough. Nobody would have to get a rifle in order to defend their town. Birdy Peach would come and take care of any problems that they might have with Sam Starr's bunch.

Still, a gloom settled over the town like none it had ever seen before. And that evening the local brass band practiced for funerals on the morrow, though none of the members had their hearts in it. The outlaws could show up at any time.

CHAPTER FIVE

Snow fell upon the freshly dug graves, turning them into what looked like lumps of sugar, and their whiteness was contrasted with that of the black dress of mourners so that it looked like there, upon the snowy and sacred cemetery grounds, a flock of crows had gathered.

Snow fell on the town, and it fell in the ditches and across the open flatness all the way to the very edge of the earth, or at least as far as a man could see. The air turned bitterly cold and crystalline so that when it was drawn into the lungs it felt like needles. Simple trips to the privy became acts of bravery and assured that the act was done quickly as possible.

Dogs curled into themselves, nose to tail, and dozed under their ruffled fur wherever they could find a place out of the wind. Children trudged to school, heads down, their faces wrapped in woolen scarves. They left deep marks in the snow where they trudged and wore their coats inside the schoolroom, along with their gloves and hats. Night winds howled like crazed women, and blew snow into blinding drifts, up to the roofs in some places.

For three days and nights it snowed, and from the unseen places in the north and in the west the wind shouted down a warning that nothing good was going to come to the people of Red Pony any time soon, that they should keep indoors and not venture forth, that they should not tempt fate. Few of them did. But there was always one who was willing to be a fool and such a man—one of the local drunks—became lost and presumed dead after three days, perhaps buried in one of the drifts, but he was of so little consequence to anyone that nobody went in search of him.

Through the rage of the storm, John Henry Cole fretted, paced, smoked cigarettes. He wished he hadn't sworn off liquor, for if there was ever a time he wanted a drink, it was while convalescing from his wounds, while listening to the storm's howl. It seemed like a portent of worse things to come unless somehow he could stop it.

He would have liked to have saddled a horse and armed himself with revolvers, a rifle, and a shotgun, and gone after Sam Starr and his gang. He would liked to have tracked them down and wiped them out entirely in order to clear the books, to even the score. But ignoring his wounds, the weather would still have stopped him. Yet Cole was not a man who could stand being idle very well at all.

The Holt & Banner stage could not get through because the roads into and out of Red Pony were impassable, and therefore Sheriff Birdy Peach and his deputy, Slade Yellowbone, couldn't get through, either. Cole knew Birdy Peach and held a reserved opinion about the man. Moreover, Slade Yellowbone was about as dangerous a man as any of those he helped Peach hunt.

There was little doubt about either man's toughness— between the two they'd probably killed a few dozen men in gunfights. In Cole's view Birdy was the lesser of the two evils, but there was something about the sheriff's demeanor that Cole didn't care for, an underlying venality, no matter that it paled in comparison to that of his deputy. Lou Ford, Red Pony's town marshal, had summoned them to come, and Cole knew as well as anyone that they would come eventually, considering the amount of reward money on Sam Starr and his gang. Notwithstanding, Cole had already allocated all that reward money once he personally caught, killed, or captured the gang. It would go to the families of his dead comrades and to Charley Hood. There wasn't so much as a nickel left over to give to anybody else.

Cole kept a rented room at Mrs. McCleary's boarding house, a temporary quarters while he was in Red Pony, but his real home was a two-day ride west across the line into New Mexico, along the Canadian River where it cut through a cañon. He'd built a small cabin there that was in a constant state of needing work, which he did whenever he found time to go there and get around to it. Mrs. McCleary was a kindly woman and a fair cook, but not a great one. She seemed to favor a lot of potatoes and not overly much meat, and when there was meat, it was usually stringy and tough. As a result Cole usually took his meals at the Morning Café.

The troubling thing was that as kindly as the widowed Mrs. McCleary was, her one and only child—a sixteen-year-old hellion named Rosetta—often took up with the wrong people, including some of the male boarders. Cole figured that the girl sold herself to whoever would pay her, did it on the sly, and knew how to use the power of her young nubile beauty. She was black-haired and coquettish, with large dark eyes and milk-white skin. Men would pay well for such a little scamp, and no doubt did. She had yet to proposition Cole, and he figured that it was not his place to tell Mrs. McCleary about her daughter. Blood was thicker than water, and, when it came down to it, sometimes those of shared blood did not want to accept the truth about their own kind.

The days turned into weeks and the weather subsided, then loosened its grip enough so a man could conduct his normal affairs. Still, you were a damned fool to venture forth with less than a good heavy Mackinaw and a pair of gloves. Cole went to visit Charley and see how he was doing.

Charley's wife Franzetta answered the door of their little rented house at the west end of town. Her countenance changed when she saw who it was standing there, and some old memory passed between them, one that neither wanted to acknowledge.

"He's not going with you again," she said angrily.

"No, I didn't come for that. I came to see how he was doing."

Charley called from somewhere within: "That you, John Henry?" Then he said: "Let him in, woman."

She stepped aside, and Cole stamped the snow from his boots and removed his hat, then entered.

Charley was sitting in a stuffed chair, his feet propped up on an ottoman covered with brown brocade with fringe around the bottom. He looked like some potentate except for the bandaged legs.

"How you making it, Charley?" Cole inquired.

"I'm making it. You want coffee?"

Before Cole could answer, Charley looked toward Franzetta and said: "Would you mind getting me and John Henry a cup of coffee with some fresh cream in it and some of those macaroons you baked yesterday? You like macaroons, don't you, John Henry?"

Cole nodded as he sat in a ladder-back rocker across from Charley. A nice fire crackled in the black woodstove in the center of the room.

"She's scared half to death I'll go with you again and come back like the others . . . Fred and them. Her and Fred's wife were awfully close, you know."

"No, I expect you'll not be going out again any time soon," Cole said.

"We come close to buying the farm, John Henry."

"We got bamboozled, that's for sure, Charley."

"There's talk running through the town that Sam and his

42

gang will come looking for us and wipe out anyone helping us."

"I heard that," Cole said. "I don't think it's going to happen. They'd be damned fools even to think it."

Charley shook his head slowly. "Knowing what I know of that son-of-a-bitch, I wouldn't put nothing past him. You two have always had sort of a vendetta against each other, ain't you?"

It was true, but what Charley and none of the others knew was that Sam was John Henry's half-brother. John Henry's mother had been widowed for two years before she met and married Jake Starr, a marriage of short duration once she learned of Jake's true nature as a wife-beater, gambler, and worse. She'd run him off with a loaded revolver, but not before she'd become pregnant with Sam. John Henry was five years old when Sam was born, and they'd grown up together until Cole went off to fight in the war. Sam was just thirteen at the time, but it was already apparent he carried his pa's bad seed in him, first showing when he began torturing cats and other animals. John Henry had whipped him several times over such behavior, and Sam had come to detest his older half-brother. It only got worse when Cole got a letter while in the war that Sam had stolen his mother's silverware and a treasured broach and run off. Cole never forgave the boy, and later when he'd learned that Sam had turned outlaw, he wasn't at all surprised. So the ambush made sense to Cole now. Sam had tracked him down and set it up.

Franzetta came in with a tray containing two coffee cups and a plate of macaroons, and set them down on a sideboard, then served them, and left the room again without saying a word.

"I don't know, John Henry," Charley said doubtfully, "but that those damn' killers wouldn't come and try and finish us. They know there's no law but Lou Ford in this town. I don't think Lou even stands up to his own wife, much less could you expect him to stand up to the likes of Sam Starr and his bunch."

"Lou sent for the sheriff," Cole said.

Charley snorted. "Birdy Peach and Slade Yellowbone? I never knew either of them to go far out of his way to help anybody if there wasn't some money in it for them."

"I know it," Cole agreed. "They'll come because of the reward money. But I already have plans for that reward money . . . for you and the others. No damned way am I going to let Birdy or Slade, either one, grab it."

Cole felt agitated, itching to do something. He didn't like sitting around and waiting. Waiting for something meant things weren't in his control, and he didn't like it. "I'm going after them," he said. "I'm patched well enough I can ride."

"How you gonna go after 'em, John Henry, when you don't have a living soul to go with you?"

"They won't be expecting it, I reckon. Maybe it's better one man than many."

Again Charley glanced toward the kitchen where his wife had gone. Seemed like, whenever Cole was about, Franzetta made herself scarce. "You know I'd go, if it wasn't for her, don't you?"

"Yes, I know you would."

"Reach over in that drawer in the desk yonder," Charley said.

Cole stood, went over, and opened the drawer to a small writing desk. In it was a pearl-handled Colt Thunderer .45 with a short blued barrel.

"You take that," Charley said. "It's a good belly gun."

"I don't need any extra guns, Charley, I got plenty."

"I know you do, but I'd like to think, if you caught them sons-a-bitches, you might kill one or two with my piece."

Cole pocketed the pistol and said: "I'll do my best, Charley."

He crossed then to where Charley sat, and offered his hand. Charley shook it, his eyes full of regret for a lot of things, not just that he wasn't going along, but for the dead and the snow and long winter cooped up in the house with Franzetta and not being able even to perform his husbandly duties. He sure enough loved her, but he loved being out on the trail more. And though it was true that he was getting on in years, and it was harder to sit a horse all day and sleep on the hard ground at night without every bone in his body hurting, he still missed not doing it. Trail grub didn't sit with him too well. It was like Franzetta said: "Sooner or later men have to stop being boys and turn themselves into something a woman can rely on." But he sure hated watching Cole go out that door alone.

"Could a feller get another damn' cup of coffee?" he called, and Franzetta appeared in the doorway of the kitchen and simply looked at him, her arms crossed under her bosom. She didn't say anything for the longest time. Then: "I know that you are wounded and hurting, husband of mine, but it gives you no right to be churlish."

"Churlish?" Charley said. "I don't even know what the hell that means, and I don't know what the hell's got you in such a state of mind, either."

She could not say, could not tell the man she was now married to what it was that had her worked up. For to tell her husband the truth would be plain hurtful and what was in the past, she told herself, should stay in the past. But it still didn't keep her from remembering, nor lessen the hurt and longing for what might have been. "It means rude in a mean-spirited way," she said, and turned on her heel, and disappeared again.

Charley shook his head and thought: *Women.*

CHAPTER SIX

Birdy Peach got the telegram and said to Slade: "Seems our services are required down in Red Pony." There was the tinge of smugness in his voice, for he had always considered himself superior to most men he knew or could name, which was just about everybody. His deputy, Slade Yellowbone, was a tall, gaunt, and hollow-eyed fellow who wasn't given much to words, and as dangerous a man as Birdy Peach had ever known. In Birdy's mind, having Slade as his deputy was sort of like keeping a fighting dog on a chain. One thing that Birdy never told anyone was that he was always fully prepared to put Slade down if it ever came to that—shoot him from behind, in the back of the head. But until that day came, Slade was a good one to take alone to a fight.

"What they need us for?" Slade asked quite casually as he looked out the window of the Beaver office, a cigarette dangling from the corner of his mouth. The view he had was of a dull gray sky that threatened more snow. He hated snow because the cold made his groin ache. Ever since that woman had shot him in Glorietta. These days, if he rode a horse or train or stage anywhere, he sat on a red pillow that had the words *HOME SWEET HOME* stitched in yellow. The only thing that would relieve his ache was cocaine pills, which he bought from a Chinamen. It had gotten so that he couldn't go more than a few hours without one. Of course washing them down with whiskey aided the effect.

"You 'member John Henry Cole, don't you?" Birdy said, gazing at the telegram.

"Sure," Slade said. "Features himself as some sort of gunfighter *extraordinaire.*"

"He *is* precisely that," Birdy replied. "He'll put a plug in you quick if you fool with him."

"So, I'm guessing he's the one who sent that?"

"No, not him. It was sent by Lou Ford, the town marshal down there. Says John Henry Cole and his bunch of detectives got their asses shot up by the Sam Starr gang. Killed three of Cole's boys and wounded him and another man. Says that the town's afraid Starr will come and burn down the town if they find out Cole's still alive and living there."

"Sounds like a bunch of yard chickens," Slade said. He had his mind on something. It was something he'd had his mind on for a long time. Why that young store clerk with those real blue eyes and those soft features kept preying on him. He kept assuring himself: *I ain't a queer duck.*

"That burg of Red Pony will never amount to nothing if the Northern don't put in a spur line. It will die and blow away," Birdy opined.

"You thinking on going?"

"I am the sheriff and it's my duty, when called."

Slade looked at his boss skeptically. "Must be some reward money in it."

"A good deal in fact now that you mention it," Birdy said with a sly smile. He spread out the Wanted posters on the Sam Starr gang and did a rough calculation of the amount to be collected if he got all of them. "I figure there's close to two thousand dollars' worth of killers just out there waiting to be had," he said. Birdy wasn't real good with numbers—toting, adding, subtracting, multiplying—but he could count to $2,000, given enough time.

Slade didn't say anything. He was thinking about what that clerk had said to him yesterday when he'd gone into the mercantile to buy a new shirt.

"Say, that will look real nice on you, Mister Yellowbone." That was just the way he said it, holding it up to him, asking why didn't he just go ahead and try it on? So Slade had taken off his old shirt and put on the new one. He had seen the way the clerk was watching him when he took off his old shirt and stood bare-chested, saying how nice he looked in that new shirt once he had put it on. Then he'd said: "You're a beautiful man, Mister Yellowbone."

No, there ain't nothing to it, the lawman told himself. But then the clerk had given him a discount, said he wasn't supposed to do it, but he wanted to because the shirt looked so good on him, and how he was meant to have it. "Oh, don't worry," Jody had said. That was his name, Jody Weatherspoon. How was it, he asked himself, that he had come to care enough to memorize that kid's name anyhow? "It will just be our little secret, yours and mine, Mister Yellowbone."

The boy had this real thick curly hair he wore long and he was slender as a schoolgirl to boot. Had hairless cheeks and a real soft tiny mouth. What first caught Slade's attention was that the boy had a limp. Like his right leg would not bend at the knee. He wanted to ask him about it, how it came to be that way, just to keep the conversation going, to justify lingering there in the store and talking to the kid some more. *Damn it, stop thinking such thoughts,* Slade told himself.

"Well?"

It was Birdy asking him something. He turned away from the window, from staring across the street at *MANGROVE'S MER-CANTILE* where the kid worked. "Well, what?"

"Well, you ready to go earn some money?"

"I reckon."

"Pack you a bag and we'll head out on the afternoon stage."

"Looks like its bound to snow."

"Well, if it does, it does."

"Might want to wait a day or two, see how this weather's gonna break."

The sheriff merely shook his head. "Time's money. Go pack."

Slade nodded, turned his eyes back to the window, to the mercantile, sighed, then left to pack, get his extra guns, and that new blue shirt. Go get himself a drink or two and see was Fanny in and available over at Ellis's Hog Palace. The afternoon stage wouldn't leave for another two hours. He had time. Time to prove there wasn't nothing wrong with him, that he was normal as any man.

So he went and he found Fanny and that time of day she was available. Slade dug out the $3 she charged and another for the bottle to take to her room with them, and he watched her get undressed as he pulled from the bottle. She was all white flesh, roly-poly, oddly enough with big thighs and small breasts. The hair under her arms didn't match the peroxide blonde hair on her head, but more than matched the dark triangle between her legs.

"You sure ain't no true towhead," he said.

"Well, hell, gunslinger, there ain't many of us genuine no more now, is there?"

"What do you mean by that?" he asked hotly. Was she insinuating something?

"Just mean to say what we once was we ain't no more, none of us."

He didn't feel a drop of desire for her but went at it anyway— fast and furious, as if the stage was due in two minutes, instead of two hours.

He said: "Gun's going off."

She said: "Go ahead and fire that thing."

49

And he did, but without pleasure, then rolled away, and pulled up his trousers and looked at her and said: "How was that?"

"That was real fine, Slade, best I ever had."

He knew that she was lying, but that was her job, to lie and make men want to crow like a rooster, so that they would return time and again. It's how a gal like her made a living, not so much by screwing but by lying.

"Tell the truth!" he demanded.

"I swear to God and Jesus, Slade. I never had it from no man like you just gave it to me. Never!"

He let it go. He wanted to convince himself that for the first time a woman like her hadn't lied to a man like him. "All right, then," he said. "Anybody ever ask you how ol' Slade is in the sack, you make sure and tell 'em I'm the best you ever had. You hear me?"

"Sure, Slade. Sure."

He stalked out and went to his hotel room and gathered his things and put them in a leather valise, making sure to keep his new shirt on top so it would not get all wrinkled. Then he armed himself with several guns and went off to the stage stop to wait along with Birdy Peach.

"Where's your pillow, Slade?"

"Shit, I forgot it."

He went all the way back to the hotel and got his red pillow, and started again for the stage stop when he nearly bumped into the clerk, young Weatherspoon, coming out of the mercantile.

"Why, howdy, Mister Yellowbone," the clerk said. "How are you?"

Slade looked at him with hooded eyes. There was something mighty tempting about that boy. Mighty tempting. "I'm leaving town for a few days," is all he said, seeing how the youth was looking at the pillow under his arm.

"Pretty pillow," Jody said.

Slade hurried on, pillow in hand.

CHAPTER SEVEN

Lou Ford was summoned to a meeting with the town council—the local businessmen, Mayor Cal Feathers, and Reverend Payworthy of the Good Pilgrims Quaker United Holiness Church. They laid before Lou their fears and said: "You go and tell John Henry Cole and Charley Hood that they must leave town as soon as possible, elsewise the Starr bunch might come and burn us out."

"Don't be foolish," Lou tried reasoning with them.

"You're the town marshal. It's your job to do all you can to protect the citizens of this town," Cal Feathers argued.

"John Henry's a friend of mine," Lou said.

"Friend or not, he must go for the good of others," Reverend Payworthy opined.

Lou saw their pitiful, worried faces and knew which side his bread was buttered on. If he refused them, they would fire him and hire another who would abide by their wishes. Lou lacked confidence in himself to find other work. He had a wife, after all.

At the boarding house, Cole knew why Lou had come and sat listening as the town marshal spoke in somber, quiet tones.

"John Henry," he began, bowler hat in hand, turning it like a plate. "The town council wants you and Charley to leave Red Pony posthaste. I hate to be the messenger, but. . . ."

He seemed to run out of breath, then words, like some steam engine with a broken belt.

"I'm willing to go, if that's what you all want," Cole said. "But Charley's stove up, shot through the legs, and I'm not so sure he's able or willing."

He watched Lou's face closely. It seemed made of putty that had set in the hot sun too long. Cole suspected that at one time or another Lou had been a man of resolve and great inner strength, but that time and marriage and other responsibilities had weakened him over the years, leaving him overly cautious, tentative, even fearful, as it does so many men. He wanted to say to Lou Ford: "When we are young, we feel invulnerable, we feel as though we can win every argument, that we can always make a case for ourselves, that nothing can deter us from our goals. But when we grow old, we lose all sense of ourselves and our dreams and our goals are but a memory as faded and fragile as a rose pressed between Bible pages. We no longer look inward, but outward for answers, and we lean too heavily on other men to bear us up." That is what he wanted to tell Lou Ford in order to brace him.

Ford continued: "We was hoping you would be the one to go and tell Charley, since he's an employee of yours. . . ."

"Best you tell him yourself," Cole said. "I'll not carry your water for you."

"Then I will do so. We'd like you to leave by tomorrow."

"So say you all?"

Lou nodded.

"You'll be the only law here," Cole said.

"We've sent for Birdy Peach. He should be arriving any day with deputies."

"So be it then," Cole said. He did not offer to shake hands. Lou stood for a moment, then donned his bowler and left.

Cole put together his bedroll. He didn't own much. He saw the accumulation of things as something unnecessary to a man of his way of life. He had always been of the mind to be ready to travel and to travel light. His days as a lawman had taught him to be ready for almost anything. You might have a job when you wake up in the morning and be put out of work by afternoon. Or it might be just the opposite. This was one reason why he'd bought the land in New Mexico—to have a place to light finally when his lawdogging days were over.

Town councils hired men to do their dirty work, to keep their towns safe, and once they got what they wanted, they got rid of the men who made them that way and hired other, gentler men who wore silk cravats and threaded waistcoats, men who carried a pocket pistol and brass watch and had clean-shaven cheeks and thoughts of someday obtaining higher office, politicians, not real lawmen.

You lived each day as if it was your last, and sometimes it was your last. Lawmen were shot by drunk boys and crazy women and hardened killers. Shot and delivered up to the bone yard—and that is sometimes how you moved on, too. But either way, you moved on. Nothing was permanent for a man who worked behind a gun. It might be a word in Mr. Webster's dictionary, but it wasn't a condition known to lawmen.

He finished his packing and sat on the edge of the bed. He fashioned himself a cigarette, then struck a match, and smoked, inhaling deeply until his thoughts lifted, carried on the airiness of the smoke itself. If the town did not want him, he did not want the town. *Maybe it's time,* he told himself. *Maybe this is a sign that it's time to hang up your guns and go live on that little place of yours and let the world alone.* But he knew that before he could let it alone, he had to take care of one last matter.

Another knock came at his door, and when he opened it, Franzetta stood with eyes wet and red.

"Come in," he said.

She did, and stood there for the longest time. "John Henry," she said at last, almost as a concession.

"Franzetta."

For another moment they breathed the air in the spartan room, and she looked about but there wasn't a lot to see—a bed, a bureau, china pitcher and bowl, both chipped, a small dark painting on the wall of a boat with men in it rowing against raging waves. Every time Cole had looked at it, he was sure those men in the boat were goners. And, of course, there were his books there on shelves. The one saving grace of a bachelor was his books, wherein he could escape to faraway worlds and peer in at the lives of others.

"The town council wants us out of town," she said at last.

"I know. Lou Ford came here first, told me to hit the road, and wanted me to tell you and Charley. I told him to do it himself. Figured they wouldn't run poor Charley and you off, him shot in the legs."

"Well, they're doing it."

The secret that only Cole and Franzetta shared was their brief past together, before Charley came to Red Pony and hired on. Franzetta had been a refugee from the East—a part of a traveling troupe of actors touring the west. She'd broken her ankle, falling off the stage, and was left behind where she eventually took work as a waitress at the Morning Café. That is where Cole had met her. There was an instant attraction between them. A fire that burned brightly, but, as such fires often do, had also burned out quickly. Franzetta was a woman with a somewhat regal bearing, had that green-eyed, imperious gaze, aquiline nose, high cheek bones. She was of an age by the time she and Cole met, when most women were married with children. But Franzetta had never been married, although she confessed to a string of lovers during their brief affair. Cole had never met such an openly sexual woman.

It was just one of those deals that happened, and they both realized it and accepted it for what it was—an encounter of two strangers who found themselves lonely and in need of something they couldn't just find anywhere. Cole had liked that she was also well read and loved the fact he had books. When it ended, the heat all dissipated, neither of them could say exactly why it had.

Cole looked at those books now, his accumulation on the shelves in his room, and knew he'd have to have them shipped to his place on the Canadian River, that they would stave off the lonely days ahead, and each time he looked at them he could not help but remember those torrid nights and seamless, languid days he'd spent with Franzetta. Even now, as she stood there, looking about, he felt a tinge of passion for her. He wondered if she, too, remembered that first night they'd spent together when they had gone back to her small rented cottage and gotten out of their clothes in the semidarkness with just enough light to see each other. And how those shadows and light had played over the graceful curves of her hips and breasts, how she had looked as if made of ivory. He asked himself how was it possible not to think such things, then as quickly admonished himself because she was now Charley's wife. In fact, it was Cole who had introduced her to Charley, and he had been only mildly surprised that Charley and Franzetta had hit it off, for they seemed like two such opposites. Charley was the same height as Franzetta and older by several years. He didn't read books. Cole wasn't even sure that Charley *could* read. Charley liked to have a good time, drinking with lots of laughter. He was always playing practical jokes, whereas Franzetta seemed reserved and humorless. But something connected them, something invisible and unknowable. And so it had been.

"I'm not sure what to do, John Henry," she said. "Charley's wounded and can barely hobble around even with crutches, and now they are kicking us out of town. God damn them for that."

"I keep a place west of here over in New Mexico," Cole said.

"It's not much, nothing fancy, but we'd be OK there, the three of us, at least until Charley can get up and around again. You're both welcome to come."

"Do you think that's a good idea, John Henry?"

"I think we don't have much of a choice," he said. "But it's up to you and Charley."

"I'll speak to him," she said, her voice now barely audible. "That won't happen again, will it?" she said as she turned and touched her hand to the doorknob. "I mean what happened before. That won't happen again?"

"No," he said. "It won't happen again."

He could not read her expression, what she was thinking when he said that. She turned and went out.

Cole made himself another shuck and smoked it as he awaited word from Charley, whether they would all leave together. Then there was that question she'd asked him, about if it would happen again between them, and he told himself that it would not, could not. But it made him fidgety, thinking it might be hard to be around her.

He checked his watch, put it away, and then checked it again. The stiffness in his side and shoulder tugged at him like teeth biting into him. But he outlasted the worst of it by pacing the room with murder still on his mind.

He had never before wanted simply to hunt somebody down and kill them. But now he did. What Sam had done was unpardonable. Becoming an outlaw was one thing, becoming an assassin who would ambush men trying to do the right thing was another. He hated himself for feeling so much anger and told himself he'd be little better than Sam were he to do that thing—hunt him down and kill him without giving him a chance. But what else was there for it?

He paced, then cleaned his guns, then paced some more, thinking to himself: *Come on, Charley, make up you damned mind*

. . . either you're going or you're not.

Cole wasn't sure but that getting shot had ruined Charley, as it did some men. Cole had seen some of the bravest men he ever knew beg and plead for their mothers or wives when they took a bullet and sensed how close to dying they were. He could understand it, but not in himself.

CHAPTER EIGHT

Preacher Man came knocking instead of Charley Hood. He stood there in his black clothing beneath a heavy overcoat of wool.

"Wanted to see how you were making out," he said. "See was there anything more I could do for you. Or, if you'd like me to pray with you."

Cole allowed him entrance. "I've no need of praying, Preacher. No offense."

"None taken. The other reason I've come is that I've been hearing rumors about the men who shot you and your friends . . . that they may try and finish you by coming here. Some are even saying that, if they come, they might burn down the entire town. Folks seem nervous about your existence."

"Nothing new there," Cole said. "I'd offer you a whiskey if I was still a drinking man, but I gave it up."

At this the Preacher Man's face changed, drew into a smile. "Well, I always keep a bit of old toss on hand," he said, producing a bottle of peppermint schnapps from within his broad coat. "Hope you don't mind?"

"Go ahead and I'll watch with envy."

Cole watched the bubbles form in the bottle as Preacher Man drank.

Two good swallows, then he plugged the neck. "Lordy!" he said, smacking his lips. "Sweet as flowering nectar. So may I ask what your plans are in light of the situation?"

"Why do you want to know?"

"I'm a man at loose ends," Preacher Man said. "Been search-ing for myself, my place in the sun for ever so long. I got a wagon and two ornery mules and thought maybe you would like to employ my services."

Fortuitous, Cole thought, *about the wagon.* He glanced at his books. Maybe he could pack them in a trunk, after all, rather than leave them. And if Charley and Franzetta came along, they'd need the benefit of a wagon as well. The thought of leav-ing at all galled him, but. . . . "How much would it take to hire you and your wagon?"

"Not much," Preacher Man said. "Dollar a day and my meals, and perhaps a couple more bottles of schnapps for those cold nights. How would that suit you?"

"Suits me fine," Cole said.

"When do you want to leave?"

"Soon as I get word back from my friend." Preacher Man stood there, and Cole could see he was waiting for something, so he took two silver dollars from a tin box he kept on a shelf by his books and handed them over. "Two dollars, two days," he said.

Preacher Man nodded. "I will be at that tavern on yon corner from here when you're ready to go."

"Good enough."

They shook hands, and Preacher Man departed.

The sun crossed from one side of the sky to the other, then slowly began to lower itself toward earth. It was a ball of red muted by the thin gray sky and shown bloodily upon the old snow. Finally Cole went to Charley's place to get an answer.

Charley opened the door, leaning on a pair of crutches, and said: "Franzetta has agreed that we go with you to your place on the Canadian. She's packing a trunk now, some of her dish-ware, particular things she feels she can't do without."

"I'm glad you're coming. We'll use Preacher Man's wagon to move."

"It ain't like we're running, is it, John Henry?"

"Call it whatever you want. It is whatever it is. But no matter what, I'm not through with that bunch, and as soon as I've got you and her settled, I intend to take care of business."

"Arrest them?"

"No, Charley, finish them."

At this Charley half smiled, for he knew that John Henry Cole was not a man to declare such things without fully meaning them. He looked back over his shoulder, then toward Cole again. "I hope to hell I'm up to it, too."

"You've done enough, Charley. You paid your wages on this one. Franzetta needs you more than I do. I'll see it done, don't you worry about that. Just get ready, and I'll come around before it gets dark, and we'll head out of this burg."

Charley nodded.

Cole handed the Thunderer to Charley. "Figured you'd want this back."

Charley nodded, but that was all.

Cole turned and went to pack his favorite books and a few other things into a small travel trunk.

Surely as the sun sank down into the far line of snowy horizon, turning the fingers of clouds that streaked the sky to a lovely crimson, Cole and Charley and Franzetta rode away from Red Pony in Preacher Man's spring wagon, the iron wheels crunching in the brittle snow following the mules' strain.

Preacher Man called to the mules and cracked the reins whenever they'd slow a bit.

"We'll make the next town . . . Pistol . . . and lay over there for the night," Cole said. "It's about ten miles up this road."

The rest of the journey into night was pretty much done in cold silence, each of the travelers wrapped up in blankets and their own thoughts. The mules seemed oblivious to everything, and Preacher Man said—"Beasts of burden, bless'd are the ignorant."—then hummed a hymn that Franzetta recognized, "Now The Day Is Over":

> *Now the day is over*
> *Night is drawing neigh;*
> *Shadows of the evening*
> *Steal across the sky.*
>
> *Jesus, give the weary*
> *Calm and sweet repose;*
> *With thy tend'rest blessing*
> *May mine eyelids close.*

Preacher Man had a fine melodious voice that soothed Franzetta's shivering soul and gave her a miniscule bit of hope. She leaned her body against Charley's and he put his arm about her shoulders and drew her near as he gazed up at the star-salted sky, the sliver of moon, and whispered: "It will be OK, love, it will be OK."

Preacher Man nipped at the schnapps, offering it to Charley and Franzetta who each nipped a little for the warmth it put into the blood. Between hymns Preacher Man looked over at Cole and said: "My mules like my singing to them . . . keeps them from becoming obnoxious."

They rode on and eventually reached the town of Pistol where they took rooms at a stark hotel knocked together of plain unpainted lumber, but were ever so glad to be in out of the black cold and resting in beds.

Cole would not allow himself to think of Franzetta and Charley in the next room or of anything other than soon wrecking revenge on his half brother, who he considered no kin at all. He knew he shouldn't rightfully feel that way, but he did. The old walls of the hotel creaked from the cold and somewhere off in another room he could hear someone coughing. And every passing minute was to him like a bitter pill to swallow. The cold made the pain of his wounds maddening and seemed to come in waves, and each time it did, he was tempted to go and find a bottle of whiskey, but he fought the urge, believing that the pain was nothing more than a necessary reminder of what he must do. He closed his eyes finally and the world went away.

CHAPTER NINE

Sam Starr was a man with a face that spoke of ruthlessness and carnage; it was youthful and feral at the same time. It was his eyes that told the true story; they were as pitiless and black as a starless night. He was honey-haired, which added to the initial deception. The creases around his eyes were grimed with the soot of a thousand campfires. Reddish-blond whorls of whisker hair graced his cheeks and chin and upper lip. To see him from a distance would make you think of a boy struggling into manhood—a dirty, restless boy. Add to this the long braid of honey-colored hair he kept tied with red ribbons and a stranger, gazing upon him, might think: *feminine*. But a closer inspection would reveal scars, nicks, and cuts from knives and fists and broken bottles. Much of his right ear had been shot away by an irate husband—a man Sam Starr had murdered simply because he could. One of the many men he'd killed.

Starr was a man who knew the taste of blood, his own and that of others. He'd once read about strange beasts somewhere in Europe, in some dark forest, who lived off the blood of their victims. It was said that such blood made these man-beasts stronger and kept them alive and that folks were afraid to leave their houses at night for fear of these beasts getting hold of them and draining their blood. Starr felt like such a man-beast. Sometimes in the bloodiest of fights, the other fellow's blood would get on him, splatter up into his face and mouth and eyes, and then he would taste it, and it tasted metallic and thickly salted like every other sort of blood, even the kind in an animal killed and eaten for supper. Well, such was blood and such were the ways of an outlaw, and Sam Starr didn't care anything about any of it one way or the other. He was what he was.

Sometimes in the darkest part of night he wept for his mother, the loss of her, his departure from her loving ways, her care. And so, too, he missed his pa, even being the son-of-a-bitch that he had been. And now and again he thought of his half-brother, John Henry Cole, how he used to envy him, but then came to hate him for cuffing him around whenever he'd do something of which Cole did not approve. One time he had hit Cole with a rock in his eye, and he had seen how that hurt Cole and it had given him a sense of power that comes with an act of brutality and he had liked the way that felt. He sometimes wondered, too, how he and Cole had ended up on the opposite sides of the law, except that God ordained it. Sam Starr, for all his sins, believed that everything was God's plan and that nobody could do anything to change what God meant for them to be or do. That's just the way it was.

It was while Cole was away fighting in the war that their ma passed, and Starr went to live with a supposed aunt over in the neighboring county—a widow whose husband had been killed in the war. It had been arranged that in exchange for her care and room and board, Starr would work her crops and do all the manly things that the husband would have done were he there. Starr, just fourteen at the time, didn't know anything about anything except that he was alone in the world, and so was she.

One night after a long hot summer day of working, hoeing weeds from the crop of corn, and other chores, the two of them were alone in that big old house, falling down around their ears. She said to him: "Little Sam, darling, you are the sweetest part of my soul and I will love you forever, in this world and the next." She'd taken to calling him by the name of her late husband. She'd been drinking dandelion wine most of that day and into the evening, and offered him some as well, explaining: "Time you come into being a man, boy. . . ." He liked the taste of the wine right off, liked the way it made him feel once it got down into his blood. Seemed like everything eventually came down to the blood.

She was a red-haired beauty to be sure, and men were always coming around, traipsing up to the cabin, knocking on the door. She'd let them in, telling Starr to go off and find something to work at for an hour or so. When he'd return, there would sometimes be money on the table that hadn't been there before. When he'd look at her, she'd say: "Don't you take to judging me, don't you damn' dare!"

That particular night they drank an entire jug of dandelion wine, then started on a second. She was dressed in a loose sack dress, nothing beneath it. He remembered, too, that she was barefooted. She had real pretty little feet. She talked on in a rambling alcohol-fueled preamble about one thing and another—about loneliness mostly, what it was like for a woman to be left alone at so young an age and how, if it weren't for the men who visited her, she did not know what she'd do to feed herself. She said that the worst was the lonely nights, even if she'd been with men earlier in the day.

"Oh, sure, there is men who come around to court me, and who would take me, but they don't want no kid that ain't theirs to raise, and I say to hell with them. Then there is the old, the halt, the lame who would marry me, but what do I want with the likes of them, Little Sam?"

He had no answer. His head was spinning. The flames in the fireplace seemed like little yellow people, dancing and hopping about. Once, he thought he saw a man's face in the window, peering in and he jumped up and ran out of the house with an old shotgun but there wasn't anybody there. He laughed and said: "I'm drunk, Aunt Jean, and so are you?"

"I won't deny it, beautiful boy," she replied.

He'd think of her and that time one cold dark night, the feel of her naked body against his, how she hovered above him, the shadows created by the firelight dancing on the walls, flickering over them like wicked tongues. The taste of her smoky wine-flavored mouth, the thickness of her tongue as it darted in and out of his mouth, not knowing what he should do, but going by instinct and her guidance. It all seemed so strange and that feeling twisted inside him like a strand of white-hot wire. Her little cries and moans, saying: "You see, boy. You see."

The very next morning she'd woke and told him he had to leave. "Go and don't come back . . . you are stained with the worst sin. You took advantage of me, your own flesh and blood. You are a sinful little bastard. Get your things and get gone and don't ever come back here!"

Her words shattered and confused. Hurt, he went away. Hurt, he found himself without anyway to sustain his life, except by hook or by crook. He had robbed an old man, beat him over the head with a chunk of firewood, left him bleeding and near lifeless. So what? Took his watch, what little money he had, a slab of bacon and two cans of beans and one of peaches. "To hell with you," he'd said, then stole the man's old horse and rode away.

Sixteen years of such activity had left him a hardened wanted man who sometimes secretly wept at night for that crazy bitch of an aunt.

The short man came into the camp's light, reported to Sam that he'd spread word that they might be coming to Red Pony, and burn that town to the ground, if they found that son-of-a-bitch, John Henry Cole, and any of his boys still alive and living there.

"You did well, Shorty," Sam Starr said.

"Damn'd if I din't," Shorty said, sitting by the fire and being passed a bottle from a case of stolen whiskey.

Four others sat around that same fire, killers every last one.

"You actually goin' ta do it?"

"Shit, what do you think?"

The one called Shorty shrugged. "What I learnt when I was back there was that some of them was kilt. Three's the number I was told, and two lived, Cole and one other, a feller named Hood."

"Charley Hood," Sam Starr said. "I know that son-of-a-bitch, too. Used to be a lawdog in Las Vegas. He kilt a friend of mine, Leo Bass. Damn him."

"I say damn that town and all them who is still alive in it, no matter the number," Black Bill pronounced. "Why waste our time and take foolish chances by going at them again, 'specially when what we could use more of is money and fun times?"

Starr looked across the fire at Black Bill. He wasn't a Negro; he was just a dark-skinned something or other. Well, maybe he was a little Negro, but more likely there was some Mexican or Cajun mixed in with his white blood. He had sort of slanted eyes like a Chinese, if that made any sense. But everybody called him Black Bill, and he didn't seem to care. He favored wearing sateen shirts and shaggy chaps and wore the brim of his hat pinned back to the crown with a big brass pin. He had fancy-stitched boots with roses on the shafts and curlicues on the toes. He claimed he had the biggest pecker west of the Mississippi, and maybe east of it, too, depending on what day he was claiming it, and how mad drunk he was. He bragged that he'd had a thousand women, maybe more. He wore a gold pinky ring on his right hand with a stone that he claimed contained a drop of Jesus's blood, and wore a silver ring on his middle left finger. He sported a brace of ivory-handled pistols—Remington break-top models of a .44-40 caliber. Big horse pistols, worn butts forward, he said, so he wouldn't shoot that big pecker off accidentally and cause a whole nation of women to go into mourning. He had an air about him that no man or woman could ever defeat him at anything. He said he had wrestled steers and once killed a bear with his clasp knife in a fight.

"Of what blood am I?" he responded to a $10 chippie's question once. "Hell, if I know or give a good god damn, I'm paying for thet beaver, not the nature of my bloodlines."

So when he said what he said about avoiding a raid on Red Pony, Sam Starr glared at him across the fire with those pitiless black eyes. "Tell me, if you could, the exact hour when you took over this gang?"

It was a challenge Black Bill felt up to. "I thought we was robbers of banks and trains and ever'thing else that had a dollar in it? When'd assassination start paying?"

Sam Starr looked around at the other faces. They were like feral dogs, eager for the taste of flesh and blood—like those creatures in Europe. "We'll take a vote," Starr conceded, knowing that leadership was a tenuous thing at best, that such men as those sitting about the fire could and would jump whichever way the wind blew. Outlaws were more independent than just about anyone else. They didn't care about rules and often did not follow anybody if they could help it. Whatever made the best sense to them at the moment was likely to get their vote. "All those in favor of going and finishing off those sons-a-bitches and maybe burning that town, raise your hands."

Only two did: Sam Starr and Shorty.

"All right then, the hell with it. We'll go rob that bank in Buffalo Jump. We'll get some money and have some fun. But after that, after we've drunk all the whiskey and pleasured all the women, then we're going to Red Pony and find those bastards we failed to kill, and kill 'em. And if they're hiding and the folks don't give 'em up, we'll burn that town so everybody knows not to fool with us any more. We'll put the fear of God into 'em. Any damn' objections to that?"

The others figured he'd probably forget about it in time. They ate a stew of beans, jack rabbit, and creek water from a big black kettle, and passed the stolen whiskey around, and Sam Starr kept thinking about what a pack of man-beasts they were.

Chapter Ten

Strange warm winds blew in from the west, causing the winter to seem like an aberration, that time was out of whack, that there was some strange cosmic doings afoot. Nonetheless no one aboard the spring wagon of Preacher Man complained about the change. They were grateful for it. And after two days' travel, they reached their destination, a sweep of land leading up to the cliffs of a cañon of the Canadian River.

It wasn't much of a cabin yet, but had a privy out back and a small corral. Stacked nearby was a load of lumber and a pile of shake shingles he'd ordered delivered on his last trip there. Cole planned on adding two more rooms.

The passengers climbed down wearily, heartened by the warm winds, and Preacher Man and Cole helped Charley along, then returned for the trunks.

"What the heck is in this one?" Preacher Man asked, groaning under the weight.

"Books," Cole said.

"Books? I'd think that perhaps guns would be more in order, considering the situation."

"Guns are in that one." Cole nodded toward another of the trunks.

Finally everything and everyone was settled inside, and Cole started a fire in the wood stove and another one in the cook stove. "We'll fix something to eat first," he said.

Franzetta volunteered to do the cooking, and began sorting

through a box of dry-goods that also contained cans of potted meat, while Cole and Preacher Man hauled up buckets of water from the nearest feeder stream of the river.

Preacher Man openly admired the place. "I bet she's pretty in the summer," he said. "A veritable Eden."

"Lots of good grass, plenty of game, good water, fish, you name it" Cole said. "Everything a man needs."

"But one," Preacher Man said.

"Oh, what would that be?"

"A woman to abide with thee."

Cole smiled. "You think?"

"Man is but half of himself without a woman to bear him along in troubled times and good."

"You seem to know an awful lot about it for a preaching man."

"Do you know what Jesus admonished?"

"I reckon He admonished quite a few things."

Preacher Man smiled knowingly. "The greatest of virtues is love. And who better for a man to love than a woman?"

"You sound like you been there."

"A time or two, yes."

"Well, I reckon if or when the time comes, there could be room for a woman here. I'm not opposed to that. This is just lonesome country, is all. It would take a special sort of woman to live out here so far from nothing."

"And children . . . ?" Preacher Man said.

"And children," Cole replied.

They had a nice but rather simple meal, made do for extra chairs by bringing in a plank of lumber and resting it across two nail kegs. Franzetta had prepared some corn dodgers, a pot of beans to go along with the potted meat, and coffee.

She sat next to Charley and across from Cole and Preacher Man whose forehead was two shades of color without his black felt hat. He was nearly bald as well.

Preacher Man had given a grace, and then they ate like wolves.

Afterward Cole and Preacher Man carried the dishes down to the feeder creek and washed them, while Franzetta and Charley retired to the single bedroom—the one addition Cole had managed to add, figuring it was indecent to sleep in the same room a man ate in or had guests in, though he'd never had any guests before this day except for Old Pablo, a neighbor a mile up the road who'd helped him some with the building when he could.

Old Pablo was a man who came and went like a ghost and rode a skinny milk-white horse with pink-rimmed eyes. Sometimes in an evening when Old Pablo had come around and helped hammer nails and saw planks and measure this and measure that, they'd sit outside and smoke cigarettes, and Old Pablo would offer to share his tequila—what he called Mexican Mustang Lineament—with Cole, but Cole, having given up drinking, would politely decline and drink black coffee instead.

Old Pablo was a man who did not say much unless he was drinking, and then he would regale Cole with stories about his youth from down along the border, meaning the border that ran along the Río Grande in Texas.

"I was a pretty bad *hombre* in my day," he would say. "I done things I ain't proud of." Old Pablo had his accent still, but Cole reveled in the fact that as a confessed illiterate Old Pablo could speak English as well as he could Spanish. It took a smart man to learn another man's language in Cole's view.

The more Old Pablo would drink, the more stories he would tell without really giving anything away that might indict him for some crime or other, knowing that Cole was once a lawman and currently a detective that mainly hunted outlaws for the reward money. It was almost as if Old Pablo was toying with him, seeing how much he could confess to without confessing to anything.

"Anybody comes around, trying to steal something or squat, I'll put some birdshot in their ass," Old Pablo had promised.

Old Pablo was heavy in shoulder and belly. He had short bowed legs, but when he was astride his skinny horse, he could appear fearsome. Old Pablo claimed he had some Comanche blood in him.

"My grandmother was Texas Comanche," he said once. "It was from her I learned to ride a horse before I could even walk. Comanches are the best horse people in the world."

Cole would drink his coffee and listen to Old Pablo tell his stories and watch the evening descend in rosy shades, the sky streaked as if a painter had made it a final testament.

"Oh how I miss them old days," Old Pablo might opine one minute, and then the very next say: "I'm glad I don't have to be chased by them Texas Rangers no more. Christ, they used to chase us all over and more than once they crossed the Río after us but didn't know the country like we did, and we'd lose them in the brush and laugh."

Old Pablo was also a man who lived alone, but, listening to his stories, Cole knew that Old Pablo had had his share of experiences with both *señoritas* and *señoras*. He spoke often of a woman named Manuella. Even related that this woman had been the wife of a fellow named Charlie Bowdre who used to run with Billy the Kid.

"You heard of him?" Old Pablo asked.

"Knew his brother, I think. Killed, wasn't he, a few years back?"

"Garrett got him. Big tall *gringo* sheriff. Gunned him down one night. Manuella told me this herself."

"Bowdre's wife?"

"His widow by then."

"Where was this?"

"Fort Sumner. You know of it?"

"No."

"Down south of here a ways. Real nice little place. The only thing is, that damn' Pecos River floods about every year and steals cattle, horse, houses, and men if they ain't careful. Even steals the dead . . . snatches them right out of their graves."

"And this Manuella?" Cole asked. "How'd you come to her acquaintance?"

Old Pablo offered what could be described as a beatific smile, that of a shy saint. "Well, you know how it is, eh, a man like I was then and a pretty widow like she was. Fate brought us together, I'd say. It's always fate when a man meets a woman and they get together, eh?"

Cole shrugged. "I reckon."

"You know what was interesting about her?"

"What?"

"Well, first she was married to this Charley Bowdre, who I never met. Garrett killed him, too. Garrett killed a hell of a lot of people, *gringos* and Mexicans. But anyway, she told me she and Billy became lovers for a bit, then Garrett killed him. And after that she had another lover, a fellow named Hector something, and somebody killed him over something. Then she met me and she was reluctant to do anything with me because she said every man she met ended up being murdered. You know what I told her?"

"What?"

"I told her it would be worth it just to spend a night with her . . . that I'd take any man's bullet for the privilege and honor."

"What did she say to that?"

Old Pablo grinned. "What do you think any woman would say to that?"

After his tequila ran out, Old Pablo would rise slowly and go and mount his horse, and ride off into the night, and Cole never knew when he might reappear again, and quite liked it that way, because one independent man understood that trait in another man.

Cole said to Preacher Man: "Looks like you and me will have to sleep on the floor."

Preacher Man said it wouldn't be his first time sleeping on a floor.

They made pallets by the wood stove and lay in its glow that filtered through the isinglass of the door and listened to the wood sap popping and the crackle as the flames ate away at the chunks of split hardwood and pine. It was a comforting feeling to lie near fire like that, to feel the heat warm on your face, to be curled like dogs in your blankets, knowing that no harm could presently reach you and whatever evil existed was beyond your door. Tomorrow would have to take care of itself. Cole closed his eyes and slept.

CHAPTER ELEVEN

Sheriff Birdy Peach and Deputy Slade Yellowbone stepped off the stage in Red Pony, the Concord finally able to get through the snow that had melted considerably under the warm Chinook winds that blew unexpectedly. One day it could be snowing furiously and the next the sun would be out with the temperature having risen into the forties. The problem was, even though the snow was melted off the roads, they had turned into a thick mire of reddish brown slather. A good six-horse team pulled them through and at last they had arrived.

"We'll go find Lou Ford," Birdy said, tapping the pocket of his waistcoat where the telegram was folded. "See if he has any new information for us."

Slade was his usual quiet, mysterious self, looking about the town and not seeing much he cared for. Red Pony was just like every other frontier town that didn't have a rail line running to it yet. Just a town built upon a promontory that overlooked a vast, treeless land that seemed to stretch out endlessly. He leaned and spat.

Birdy didn't see anything he cared for either with regard to the town. It was too cold in the winter and too hot in the summer and not a tree tall enough to hang a man from anywhere in sight. If you wanted to hang a fellow, you'd best do it from a telegraph pole—just put a rope around his neck and fling it up over a crossbar, then dally the other end around a saddle horse, and haul the sucker up. The sheriff had seen it done and it was no way to hang a fellow properly, watching him strangle slowly, kicking his feet and flopping around like a caught fish. And thinking of fish, Birdy figured maybe once they got all that Starr bunch's reward money, he'd quit the territory and head for Colorado where he'd maybe write his memoirs—something he'd already begun doing privately, keeping a journal of major events in his life, of the famous and infamous men he'd encountered. Men like Buffalo Bill that one time, and an aged Kit Carson, who was this little bitty fellow not more than five feet tall who'd walked all over the West and fought every kind of wild Indian. To look at Carson, you'd think he couldn't fight his way out of a whorehouse with a pair of Dragoon pistols. But he had those fierce eyes and a hawkish face and a real bloody history, so men gave him a wide berth, even in his old age. And since Carson and others, along with the United States Army, had tamed most of the Indians, the mountains were safe to go into and that made them all the more charming to Birdy. Why he could just see himself every morning sipping his coffee while he cogitated, pencil in hand, with maybe some pretty little chippy close by, willing to do his bidding and fulfill his carnal desires.

Birdy was familiar with Red Pony, having been there before, the last time to pick up a prisoner and deliver him to the jailhouse in Ardmore, so he knew Lou Ford first-hand. He thought Lou to be a tad on the soft side for a lawman.

Birdy and Slade stayed to the board sidewalks to avoid tramping through the thick red mud, their boot heels knocking on the boards as they walked, squeezing past folks headed their way, Birdy touching his hat brim to the ladies, Slade ignoring them, his thoughts elsewhere. His ass felt like it was on fire after that long, rugged, arduous stage ride, on which it seemed the driver had hit every rut and chuckhole in the road. He reflected he should best stop at the druggist and get some laudanum or cocaine pills.

They found Lou Ford just coming out of his office—a narrow wood structure that housed a two-cell jail. Lou had started for his home to have lunch with his wife Katy when he saw Birdy and Slade coming up the walk, Slade with a pillow under one arm and carrying a big bore rifle in his hand. Lou stopped and waited for them, knowing he'd have to hold off on lunch until his business was conducted with Birdy and Slade. He sure had his mind set on lunch because usually, right after, he and Katy took a little nap together and sometimes one thing led to another. He sort of had that in mind today.

"Sheriff," Lou said upon spotting Birdy and Slade. Slade frightened him a little, like some men did, even though he was a lot bigger and heavier a man than Slade. But size didn't have anything to do with it, sometimes.

"What's the latest with your expected troubles?" Birdy said.

Lou shrugged, almost helplessly. "It might just be a rumor somebody started, or it could be that the Starr bunch is really coming. Figured we might be able to use some law down here besides me. I've got no deputies."

"Why ain't you?" Birdy asked.

"They up and quit soon as they heard Sam Starr and that bunch might be coming."

"Damn' pussy willows," Slade said.

"Did manage to talk John Henry Cole and Charley Hood and his missus into leaving town, so, if Sam does show up, at least we can say is that they're not here and leave us be."

"You aim to add pretty please?" Birdy said.

Lou shifted his weight, uncertain as to why they were prodding him.

"I never thought John Henry Cole would tuck tail and run," Birdy went on. "You, Slade?"

Slade stood, stiff as a board, his back shifted now to the wall of the boot shop behind him, as was his wont. There had only been one man that Slade had ever met that he truly admired: Wild Bill Hickok. Slade had been a kid when he saw Hickok gun down Dave Tutt in the town square in Springfield. Five years later as a young man trying to make his own reputation, Slade watched as Hickok was jumped by two soldiers in a saloon in Hays City. It was a desperate if brief fight, Hickok nearly being murdered, but he had managed to shoot both men. How it came to pass that Hickok ever let anyone get behind him and shoot him in the back of the head up in Deadwood was still a source of wonder to Slade Yellowbone. The Wild Bill he'd known was forever cautious and quick to kill anyone who threatened him. But men like Slade knew it only took one second of inattention to your surroundings and those in it to earn you a bullet to the brain. His eyes drank in every living soul on the street.

"Slade?" Birdy repeated.

"What?"

"You ever think a man like John Henry Cole would tuck tail and run?"

Slade looked at him then, those pitiless eyes just like staring into a rattler's, Birdy felt. "I never thought a lot of things," Slade said. His mind was still on queer doings, that clerk and himself. What sort of man would his mean old daddy say he was if he knew what Slade was thinking about? His old man had been as hard as aged hickory, a two-fisted drinking son-of-a-bitch who would and did fight anybody at the drop of a hat, but he'd get down on his knees every Sunday in the local Baptist church and howl like a dog in praise of the Lord—rough as a cob, mean as a snake, and pious as a saint. Slade had also seen his daddy whip his ma like a rented mule, beat her right down to the ground, using his belt on her over the slightest perceived infraction. Slade's daddy was the first man Slade had ever killed. Slade had caught him with a woman in a grove of pomegranate trees, the woman bent over, her skirts hiked up, and her hams bare, the old man plunging into her, causing her to yelp and holler. Slade had gone out hunting squirrel and rabbit and whatever else he could find for the supper pot—the old man too uncaring even to put food on the table. Slade had watched him for a time, watched him go at it hard with the woman until he finished up. Slade had seen then, when she straightened up and brushed her hair off her face, that she was the neighbor's wife— Becky Barlow, old Tillis's wife, and ugly as sin. He had seen his daddy hand her a coin he took from his pocket. Where'd he gotten the money for a poke was what got to Slade the most.

Soon as she'd left to go back to her home, Slade had put the bead of his front sight right on his pa's pumpkin head and called to him: "Daddy!"

The old man had wheeled around, trying to see where the voice was coming from. Slade had stepped into the clearing. He had wanted him to see who it was who was going to kill him. Instead of acting frightened, the old man had cursed him, called him a son-of-a-bitch, said: "Should have kept the leavings running down your ma's leg and tossed you away, boy."

"Yeah, you should have," Slade had said, and pulled the trigger.

The slug hit home with the impact of a sledge-hammer against a ripe melon and blew blood and brains into a spray that coated the fresh green grass. The old man had fallen with a thud, dead and unmoving for evermore.

"There you go," Slade had said, and felt through the old man's coveralls for any more money and found $5.

Slade had gone home and gotten a shovel. He went back and buried the old man, putting brush and rocks over the spot so nobody would stumble across it accidentally, then had given the money to his mother and packed a bedroll and gone away.

Killing a fellow wasn't nearly as hard as he had thought it

might be. In fact, knowing he could take a life so easily was a special sort of feeling Slade imagined most men would never experience. And later he understood about Wild Bill, how he acted so coolly in a fight, how he tended to shoot first and ask questions later. Later was always a good time to ask questions. Slade also figured that to kill in the name of the law was the best way there was to take another man's life. That star and the gun to go with it were a coronation of sorts, sanctioned by the government.

"Well, I never figured he would," Birdy continued about his amazement over Cole's having left. "But him being gone is less competition for us on that reward money, ain't it, Slade?"

Slade nodded, only half interested in what Birdy had to say.

"Which direction did Cole encounter them assassins, Lou?"

Lou told him about the place, the orchard, what he'd learned about it, and pointed out the direction.

"Best we lay over for a night, and then get a start in the morning," Birdy said.

"Sure, Birdy, whatever you say," Slade replied, anxious to get this latest business over with so he could get back to Beaver.

Lou Ford watched them cross the street, heading toward the small hotel, the mud clinging to their boots, and begrudgingly admired them for their killer ways. Birdy Peach might sound like the name of a man you'd not think was someone you'd have to concern yourself with, but he had killed any number of men since becoming sheriff. Lou had heard plenty of rumors that dead was how he preferred bringing them in, him and Slade both. Lou felt half sorry for Sam Starr and his bunch if Birdy caught up with them.

The marshal turned and headed for his and Katy's little rented house. She'd wonder why he was late for lunch, and whatever else they might end up doing that day, Lou was glad he didn't have to go after any outlaws.

CHAPTER TWELVE

The new day dawned, bright and clear, like crystal glass. Snow lay in patches over the ground like torn pieces of a wedding dress. The air was so cold it felt like it would break. John Henry Cole and Preacher Man stirred from their pallets, and Cole set about stoking life into the glowing embers of the wood stove, adjusting the flue.

"We need some more wood," he said.

Preacher Man hurriedly dressed against the chill in the room, blowing on his hands. "Wind knows how to find you in this place," he said without coming straight out and commenting to Cole on his carpentry skills. There were cracks, both visible and invisible, that the chill wind found with no trouble at all.

It had been some time since Cole had been able to work on the place. While not quite into ruin, the cabin would still require a lot of effort just to make it soundly livable, especially with winter setting in.

Cole and Preacher Man went outside to the woodpile of thick, sawn logs Cole had stacked from his last visit the autumn before. He had felled several hardwood trees down in a cañon grove a few miles north, he and Old Pablo, working together with a bucksaw, but they hadn't enough time to get to the actual splitting part. The wood needed splitting now, but Cole knew he'd have a hell of a time hefting an axe and swinging it very hard into stove wood.

"Let me have a hand at her," Preacher Man said, and set to work.

Preacher Man put everything he had into it, brought the axe down, hard and true, and every piece yelped in protest as it split open and fell apart. Sometimes the piece would stick to the cold blade when it was too thick and knotty, and Preacher Man would heft it into the air and bring the whole shebang down a second time to crack it apart. Grinning, he said—"Firewood burns twice."—as heat from the labor worked its way up his arms and into his shoulders, and he had to stop at one point and remove his coat, fold it nicely, and put it on the ground. He rolled up both sleeves past his elbows and busted that wood as well as any man Cole had ever seen, including himself.

Cole built himself a cigarette, lit it, and smoked, watching Preacher Man, wondering what sort of soul he was, truly. But Preacher Man's secrets were his own to keep, like any man's, and he found that by throwing himself so fervently into a task, be it preaching or splitting wood, he did not have to think so much about past times, losses, and old regrets.

There was something in seeing that wood split in two, the way it would fall apart reluctantly, one to each side that reminded Preacher Man of children, the issue of his own loins, that tragic night so very long ago that he'd forgotten exactly the number of years, just that it was about this same time of year, and brutally cold outside. Preacher Man had not been a preacher then. He'd been more or less a drunk, a besotted man with a wife and too few dollars, a man with plenty of bad habits and wanton ways.

He'd been young and had fallen in love with a bewitching woman named Marvis Belle Lewis, and they'd lived in St. Louis, Missouri in a little house that had a view of the muddy waters of the Mississippi River. Marvis had been one of those so-called "good bad women" that honest folks always spoke of. She truly did have a heart of gold and loved Preacher Man as if he was a pretty child. She helped support him and his bad habits and put up with his carousing and gambling and drinking. Preacher Man, in spite of every vow he'd ever taken never to become a fool for any woman, became a fool for Marvis Belle Lewis.

It wasn't planned, but after a short time she'd become pregnant and had grown awfully big in the belly. A woman friend of Marvis's said she'd have twins. It gave Marvis Belle Lewis a glow, but more than that, it seemed to change her, turn her into a more or less a God-fearing woman who began visiting the local church twice a day.

"You'll have to get work," she'd said to Preacher Man. "I can't go back into the cathouses."

He was willing to do anything for her, even if it meant dealing from the bottom of the deck, or knocking a drunkard over the head and picking his pockets. The babies came prematurely and the doctor had to cut Marvis's belly open with a scalpel that went through her swollen flesh as easily as a razor through warm butter. Preacher Man, forced to help, had held the mask that the medico dripped ether into, then helped sop up the blood as it spilled from the cutting. It seemed cruel and unnatural to him, murderous.

"They won't come natural," the physician warned. "Have to cut them babies out."

It seemed to Preacher Man the devil was at work. "Stop!" he yelled at the medico.

"We have no choice," the physician said. "Either this or your woman and those babies will die."

It was such a bloody mess. And as if to complete the sinister aspect of it, the fetuses were co-joined at the base of their tiny little skulls.

"Oh, dear God," the medico had exclaimed as he pulled free

the barely alive infants. Their little chests rose and fell weakly. There would have been no saving them, he would explain later as he washed his stained hands in a basin of clear warm water upon their expiration. "They wouldn't have had no kind of life even if by some miracle they had survived," he had said.

Together the twins were no larger than a pair of garden squashes.

"I'm sorry, young man, it just wasn't meant to be. It went against Nature."

Marvis lingered for several fevered days, then slowly her soul was released to go and join the spirits of her children. Somewhere in a white and golden heaven she did believe in her final lucid thoughts, they would be there waiting for her.

Preacher Man stayed drunk for nearly a year, more besotted than ever. He got so bad that he was run out of every place he went into, like some cur dog nobody wanted around. He was arrested several times for loitering, drunk and disorderly, disturbing the peace, picking pockets. He was warned by the local police to leave St. Louis, or else. And when he failed to go, the police drove him across the bridge and dumped him off on the other side of the river with a stern warning that, if he showed his face again, they'd send him to prison—or kill him.

He wandered for a time until he was broken upon the wheel of life and reached a point where he put rocks into the pockets of his ragged coat and walked into the river to drown. But even that failed him, for a man came along and pulled him right out of his coat and dragged him onto the muddy bank.

"Why'd you save me?" he'd asked the man when he sobered again.

The fellow was of middle age with long, flowing hair that was pure white—too white for a man his age—and steely blue eyes. "You'll die soon enough, Hobart," the man had said. "No sense in rushing it."

"How'd you know my name?"

The man did not answer that particular question, but instead had handed him a piece of crisply fried chicken he'd been turning on a stick over a small fire he'd built there under the bridge. It had begun to rain but they'd stayed nice and dry under that bridge.

"I'd just as soon be dead as anything," Preacher Man had said. His true name was Hobart Cain, but of a long since lost lineage, for he knew not where any of his people were, so long had he wandered. He knew he had an aunt and uncle and some cousins somewhere, but it was a dreamy nameless place wherever they were.

"We each of us have a purpose to be served," the fellow had said. "How's that chicken?"

"Don't feel none like eating. You got a drink of something hard?"

The man had shaken his head. "Don't drink."

"Why the hell not?"

The man had offered a wry smile. "Because if it helped anything, I would, but it don't, so I don't."

"Maybe not, but sometimes it sure feels like it does."

"It's merely an illusion, like a lot of things we come to believe but are not true."

"What is truth?" Preacher Man had said without knowing why he said it.

"Good question. Maybe someday you'll find out."

"Someday? Mister, I don't plan on living until tomorrow."

"Doesn't matter what you plan," the man had said, gnawing on a fat drumstick and licking his fingers.

"Why don't it?"

" 'Cause each of our days is numbered in a book . . . yours different from mine, mine different from the next fellow's. When it's your time, you'll go, same as me, same as everyone. You'll go whether or not you want to, and there's nothing can be done to prevent it. But till that time . . . you might just as well make good use of the time you're allotted."

The river whispered within its banks, a low slippery sound, and somewhere farther out in the middle a big fish splashed. Or, was it a turtle?

"What's your interest in all this?" Preacher Man had asked. "Why don't you just let folks to their own devices? I want to finish myself, what business is that of yours?"

"None in particular," the man had said, holding out the other drumstick for Preacher Man to take. "Except, I am avowed to be my brother's keeper."

"Brother? I never see you before in my life," Preacher Man had said, aggrieved somewhat, but taking the proffered drumstick nonetheless. He reckoned he hadn't tasted anything so good in a real long time as that piece of charred chicken.

"We are all of the same family, Hobart, you and me."

"What family would that be?" he had said churlishly, for he was growing weary of such fancied talk.

"Why the family of man, of course."

Well, that somehow struck him in a way he hadn't expected to be struck, like a hot nail spiked into his core. "You're talking pure nonsense," he had said.

"Don't believe me?"

"No, I damn' well do not."

"Then go and finish what you started before I came along."

He had seemed awfully cocksure of himself, this stranger.

"Hell if I won't."

The fellow had been leaning on one elbow, eating quite leisurely and did not protest or try and stop him from walking back into the river. Preacher Man had stood and gone to the edge and stopped and looked back, but when he did, there wasn't anybody there, just the fire and some chicken bones.

"Hey!" he had shouted. "Hey! Where'd the hell did you go?"

No answer. He had looked at the river, then back again to the fire.

"Am I dreaming? Am I dead?"

No answer.

Just there alone, standing at the river's edge, the water flowing nice and slow, waiting for Preacher Man to step in. No matter what he did, Preacher Man realized the river would always flow and nothing would change without him in it—that life would go on as it always had and always would and not a single thing to mark his coming or leaving. He had gotten dizzy. Then he had gotten scared. Then he had found the little Bible he did not recall seeing before, right there where the man had been reclining. He had thought it a sign that he should change his ways, seek another answer. That the answer he had been seeking was not to be found in the bottom of that muddy Mississippi River, that it was somewhere else—somewhere out there in the great beyond.

So he had taken up the Bible and begun reading by the light of that fire, and sucking the marrow from those chicken bones and suddenly life never tasted so sweet, nor seemed to hold so much promise. And it was right there in Romans: *For I am unashamed of the Gospels, for it is the power of God for salvation to everyone who believes.* There was no thunder crashing from the sky, no strange voice, no calamitous event, just the words in that worn old Bible and some cooked chicken. That's what he'd later tell those he would bear witness to about the turnabout of his life from sin and ruin.

"Nothing quite like a good meal of fried chicken and a little bit of the Lord's word to set a man on the righteous path," he'd say.

He never knew from day to day where he'd be, what he'd eat, how he'd make out, but somehow he always did—like now, here with these good folks, helping out as he could, letting tomorrow take care of itself. He chopped that wood like he was chopping down Satan's house, and stacked it neatly there beside the door for hauling inside.

"Right nice work, Preacher Man."

"Whatever I put my hand to, I try and do my best," Preacher Man said. "Speaking of which, I'd like to offer you a proposal."

"I'm listening."

"Seeing as how both you and Mister Hood are recovering from your wounds, perhaps you could use my help around here until you get back to full bore."

"Couldn't afford to pay you, Preacher Man."

"No pay required. It is enough for a decent meal and roof over my head."

"Thing is, it might get bloody around here before all is said and done. I don't think you'd want to get caught up in my and Charley's troubles."

"Trouble and me are no strangers, Mister Cole."

There was something about him that caused Cole not to doubt what he was saying. "Well, it's a free country and if you want to hang around, be advised that it could get damned dangerous and you might have to end up taking a life to save your own."

"Thy days are numbered, like the hairs on my head," Preacher Man said. "Think I'll take a walk and look around."

"Suit yourself," Cole said, and watched him go, then hauled in some of the wood, as much as he could easily carry.

Cole set some pieces of wood in the stove and lit a fire in the cook stove so Franzetta could set about preparing breakfast.

"Where's Preacher Man?" Charley said.

"He's out taking a stroll," Cole replied. "Chopped a good load of wood like he knew his business."

"Not afraid to get his hands dirty, is he?"

"More than that," Cole said. "He asked if he could stick around for a time."

"He realize we might be in a jackpot?"

Franzetta looked skeptically over her shoulder.

"He does," Cole said.

"Might not hurt to have an extra . . . ,"—he almost said gun, but then thought better of it because of Franzetta—"hand."

"Couldn't hurt."

They had breakfast, but Preacher Man hadn't yet returned. Cole and Charley went outside to smoke and keep an eye on things.

"Soon as you're up to it," Cole said, "I want you to take Franzetta and get the hell gone from this country."

"What kind of a man would I be to leave you here to face them if they come?"

"A smart one," Cole said. "And don't argue. You'd be doing it for her."

Charley grumbled a bit, but he didn't outright protest what he knew was the right thing to do.

"Besides, I got Preacher Man now."

"Preacher Man?" Charley said skeptically.

"He'll do," Cole said.

"I reckon he'd better."

Then Cole said: "What's that?"

Charley looked to where Cole was looking, away out across the valley. "I don't see nothing," he said.

"It's a rider coming," Cole said.

"Rider?"

Charley looked as hard as he could. He still didn't see anything.

"Coming straight toward here," Cole said.

"It's them?"

"No, it's just one man."

It took several minutes before Charley saw the rider, too. "I see him now."

"He's coming straight toward us, isn't he?"

"He is."

"Better get inside, get Franzetta down on the floor, safe," Cole said, drawing his self-cocker, thumbing open the gate, and checking the loads, before slipping it back in his holster.

"Awful early for a killing," Charley said, swinging about on his crutches.

"You tell that to whoever that is when he gets here," Cole said.

"What about Preacher Man? He's still out there somewhere."

"Preacher Man will have to fend for himself."

Charley went inside, told Franzetta to go into the back room and get down under the bed, then he got his Winchester and took up a position by the window where he could see out across the valley.

The rider rode a funny-looking horse—the front half brown, the back half white, like somebody had given it a bad paint job.

He'll never sneak up on anybody with that horse, Charley thought.

CHAPTER THIRTEEN

It had begun to snow in big white fluffy flakes the morning the six of them rode into Buffalo Jump—three of them came in from the north and the other three from the south so as to not raise any alarms about seeing six armed men, riding into town together.

"Might as well wave a red flag and show your ass, we ride in all together," Sam Starr had said. He featured himself as a planner, a man who knew how to rob a bank and get away clean.

"It looks like there can't be more than ten dollars in the entire place," Shorty grumbled.

Atticus Creed rode slightly behind, his fingers cold already from the weather. He was not a man of many words. He just wanted to get in and get it over with.

"Maybe we should rob the saloon instead," Shorty suggested. "Least we'd get drinks and some luncheon meats."

Black Bill, Pat Gunnerson, and One-Eye rode in from the north. They rode silently, leisurely, as if just coming into town for breakfast—just three hands off some nearby ranch somewhere. Under their coats were plenty of pistols; each man had at least two; Black Bill had four in total. Each also had a Winchester rifle, as did those riding in from the south. Between them they had enough guns for a small army. The streets were mostly empty of human activity at that time in the morning, and with the snow falling and weather threatening, there wasn't much point of getting out of bed if you didn't have to.

Juno Fly had just taken the *CLOSED* sign out of his barbershop window and put up the one that read *OPEN,* and now sat in his barber's chair, drinking a cup of coffee and looking over the Sears, Roebuck catalogue. He was especially interested in bicycles. He had this crazy notion of trying to ride a bicycle across the continental United States. It had never been done before as far as he knew. He did not know why he wanted to do it, just that he did. He was a bachelor for one thing, no wife or family to care for, nothing to prevent him from going on a grand adventure. He had practically grown up in this same barbershop—his father's, which was now his. His father had taught him the art of cutting hair, had practically pontificated on the merits of being a barber, of owning your own business, of being known around town as a solid citizen who could be relied on always to do his civic duty. Juno Fly was forty-five years old the day Sam Starr's gang rode into town. Forty-five years old and imagining himself riding from the Atlantic Ocean to the Pacific, of being fêted by huge cheering crowds as the first man ever to ride a bicycle clear across the county. His eyes affixed on a Penny Farthing in the catalogue, and his dream grew large. *Damned if I'm not going to do it,* he thought. *Damned if I ain't.*

Emile Fritz was also getting ready to open his butcher shop. Game hunter Wallace and his boy Thad were expected to come by later. They'd probably have two or three deer, maybe a nice fat brown bear. On which the butcher would make a tidy profit once he dressed out the meat to sell to the townsfolk. His wife Eva was still in the back apartment, sleeping. She was a robust woman of enormous appetites and had once been a pretty slender girl when they'd met back in Berlin. But she'd long since grown and grown into what she was now, hardly recognizable from what she was then. In ten short years she'd gone from pretty and petite to big and brutish, and as strong as Emile.

94

Emile went about with a heart longing for Eva to be beautiful again, and whenever an attractive lady from the town came into his shop to buy meat, he would sigh and wink and be quite amenable. He was the second to see the trio of riders. Two of them had bearded faces and one looked like a colored man. They rode big chestnut horses, like what Emile had ridden in the cavalry way back during the war. Their winter coats were shaggy and Emile saw that each man had the stock of a rifle sticking from a scabbard. He was distracted only briefly before returning to carving up a side of beef that had come in late yesterday.

Beyond the butcher and the barber, no one else had spotted the gang. The six riders met in front of the small stone bank. Sam Starr, Shorty, and Black Bill dismounted, according to plan, while the others sat their horses. One-Eye held the reins of the dismounted horses while Pat Gunnerson and Atticus Creed kept watch in either direction of the main street, ready to shoot down anyone who might oppose them.

Inside the bank, Harley Smith and Cal Mann had finished counting the money in their money drawers and Mr. Gottlieb had finished dialing open the vault. They looked more than a little surprised to see that their first customers of the day planned a big withdrawal.

"Hands high, boys, and this can get done without shedding a drop of blood, most of which will be yours."

All three customers were holding pistols, cocked and aimed. Black Bill jumped the cages and quickly put the barrel of his pistol to Mr. Gottlieb's head.

"Fill up these pokes, hurry now," he said, pulling two burlap onion sacks from inside his coat. "Don't make me shoot you in the brains."

Sam Starr and Shorty followed suit, producing their own burlap sacks for the tellers to fill.

"No coins," Sam Starr ordered. "Too damn' heavy."

Money was dropped all over the floor out of sheer nervousness. Mr. Gottlieb's hands trembled as he did his best to fill the sacks, knowing that the money he was filling them with belonged to good, hard-working, respectable folks. He was wont to twist that gun from the dark-skinned fellow's hand and beat him over the head with it, but he'd lost his nerve from the first instant.

"Hurry up, you cabbage-headed old fool," Black Bill ordered.

"I . . . I. . . ."

For a moment, it seemed like the business being conducted was legitimate, that the transactions were of a normal order, that money was simply being exchanged from one set of hands to another. Then suddenly there was a burst of gunfire from outside and a bullet shattered a neat hole through the front window, followed by shouts and curses. The cause of it was that Juno Fly had gotten up to get himself another cup of coffee from the stove by the front door, looked across the street, and seen three fellows, sitting their horses right outside the bank, and he noted that one of the fellows was holding the reins to three empty, saddled horses. Juno forgot all about that Penny Farthing bicycle he'd been looking at and went and got the shotgun he kept in the backroom. It was an old Whitney double-barrel with rabbit-ear hammers. He kept it loaded with double-ought buckshot. He had exited the barbershop and run to the butcher shop and shouted to Emile Fritz: "They're robbing the bank, get your gun!"

Emile kept a carbine he'd carried in the war as a cavalryman, a Spencer. Together, like fools, they had run out onto the walk and started firing at the riders in front of the bank. Emile's bullet had gone through the bank's front window, and he said: "Holy Chessus!"

Juno cut loose with both barrels of the scatter-gun and saw one of the saddle horses that fellow was holding rear up on its hind legs and topple over dead. The gunfire alerted others in the town, and they knew to grab their guns, that something was up. The priest down at the church started ringing the church bell. Another call to arms—either fire or some like disaster was occurring on the streets of Buffalo Jump.

Pat Gunnerson and Atticus Creed promptly wheeled their mounts about and charged across the way, and between them shot Emile and Juno a dozen times. The old friends danced and spun like marionettes in the hands of a palsied puppeteer, then fell dead as if the puppeteer had cut their strings—snip, snip.

"Dumb sum-bitches," Pat Gunnerson said.

In their last fully conscious moments, Juno saw himself riding a Penny Farthing into the sea, and Emile saw his sweet wife, young and slender again. Then all became forever blackness.

Gunnerson and Atticus Creed wheeled their mounts back around, firing wildly at anything or anyone who moved along the street. One-Eye had let loose of the reins of Black Bill's dead horse as his own mount wheeled around and around as if trying to escape, but he kept control of it and the other two horses he was still holding.

Townsmen took up positions from within buildings, behind windows, one behind a water barrel, another in the bed of a parked wagon—anywhere they could fire from and not be fired upon. The air crackled with gunfire and gunsmoke formed tiny storm clouds.

Sam Starr and Shorty and Black Bill came running out of the bank, money in onion sacks gripped in their hands. Bill saw that his horse was shot down and jumped on behind Shorty, and the gang of them rode through a withering fire that seemed to be coming from everywhere at once.

One-Eye took a bullet in a leg and yelped, but his yelping was not heard above the racket of gunfire. Black Bill had his hat shot off and it left his ears ringing so that it sounded like he'd gone into a tunnel. Pat Gunnerson got shot clean out of the saddle, hit by a dozen slugs as if he was the main prize in a shooting gallery. It could have been the fancy sombrero he wore and the leather britches that attracted the gunfire. His left foot got hung up in the stirrup, and the town fighters continued to pour lead into him as he flopped along dead as a yanked carp. When it looked as if he might be dragged clean out of town, the citizen shooters shot his horse to make sure it did not escape with the corpse.

But the rest got away and disappeared into the surroundings like smoke in the night. They rode hard and got lost in some arroyos that were deep enough to hide them and kept going until darkness fell. They wondered aloud that night how it was they had survived at all—everyone except Pat Gunnerson. Gunnerson was currently displayed, bound with bobbed wire to a door taken off the barbershop, which seemed only appropriate seeing as how the barber had been killed, gunned down with the butcher, both them called brave men and mourned.

A posse had been quickly formed, but composed of men not used to tracking or finding killers, and by dusk they had returned to Buffalo Jump, just as glad not to have encountered the desperate outlaws. Another victim had been the Tolvard kid who'd run to look at what was happening. Someone had shot him through the neck and he'd bled to death, but no one could truly testify if the kid had been shot by outlaws or enraged citizens, so of course the kid's murder was laid at the feet of Sam Starr's bunch—recognized by the old-time constable, Lazlo Metz, who'd seen and knew by sight just about every bad man in the Cherokee Outlet. He quickly wired for Birdy Peach. The wire, when arrived in Beaver, was forwarded to Red Pony by the telegrapher. Lou Ford tracked down Birdy and Slade having breakfast, and handed it to them.

"Looks like our boys have hit a bank in Buffalo Jump," Lou said.

Town of Buffalo Jump raided this day. STOP. Three citizens murdered. STOP. Come quick. STOP. May have been the Sam Starr gang. STOP. Lazlo Metz, Constable, Buffalo Jump, OK TERR.

CHAPTER FOURTEEN

Whoever the rider was, he sat a good horse, riding at an easy lope, one arm loose along his side, the other holding reins, he and the horse in rhythm as if they were one creature instead of two.

"I got you covered from in here, John Henry," Charley said through the crack of the window he'd pried open. "Say the word and I'll put some lead in him."

"Hold your fire until we see what's what," Cole said.

"You see any sign of Preacher Man anywhere?"

"Not yet."

"He probably went and got himself lost in that daydreaming state of his."

Cole watched as the rider came steadily on, closing the half-mile gap easily enough. The horse was an Appaloosa, big-muscled chest, head held high and proud, not like any Appaloosa Cole had ever seen before. It seemed to glide over the ground.

When the rider got close enough Cole could see that he was slightly built, dressed in a canvas coat over a corded sweater, dungarees, and rough brown boots with low heels. Hiding the rider's face was the flop brim of a low-crowned black hat that had seen better days, stains of white sweat riming the crown. Cole could see, too, the butt of a Winchester poking from the boot under the rider's right leg.

He reined up, and the horse stood still except for the ripples under its muscled hide. Cole waited for the fellow to speak.

"Looking for John Henry Cole," the fellow said, then thumbed his hat back far enough so that Cole could see his face, see that he was a young man. There was something familiar about him even underneath the dark beard and mustache gracing his face.

"Who's asking?" Cole said.

"I'm asking," the rider said, real cocky.

"You never said a name," Cole returned. "Don't know you."

"I see your man in the window yonder, and that one over near the shithouse."

"Preacher Man!" Cole called.

Preacher Man stepped forth from behind the privy, a sweet little nickel-plated revolver in his hand. He tucked it away in his waistband as Cole gave him the signal to put it away.

"Put your rifle down, Charley!" Cole called over his shoulder. "I don't think this boy has come to assassinate us. Or, have you?"

The kid opened his coat, and when he spread it apart, Cole saw the butt-forward pistol worn in a cocked leather holster, the way a shootist might wear it. "No, I don't reckon I rode all this way to kill you, John Henry Cole."

"You figured it out then."

"Yeah," the rider said. "How'd I ever forget, though you've put on heft some and gotten old."

"That a fact?"

"She wanted me to come find you and let you know she's dead."

"You make no sense."

"Tom, is how you'd remember me. That's what you named me, or she did. Never got the story quite straight."

Then John Henry Cole knew—it was his son by Anna Rain, back in the Nations, a long time ago. He hadn't seen the boy in ten years, and now here he was a full-grown man. The last time he'd seen Tom was when he took him from the outlaw gang he'd fallen in with and delivered him back to Anna. He'd aimed to come back to them, and in fact had, but they had fled. Some who knew them said north to Canada. Cole had gone in search of them both but had lost their trail. They had simply disappeared. And now here was Tom returned, much like the prodigal son.

"You said she wanted me to know she was dead?"

The rider nodded. "Up in Alberta she got real sick and begged me to bring her back to the Nations, which I did, but she died a day short of getting to her old home grounds. Buried her in Tahlequah. She had me promise to track you down and let you know. And so I have."

"Step down from your horse and set a spell, if you would," Cole said, still shaken by the news. Tom was his second son, his first having died in infancy along with his wife, years and years ago. Tom was the result of a brief liaison with the Cherokee woman when he was still an U.S. marshal. It was brief in time only due to the fact that Anna hadn't told him she was pregnant and then she later married. But brief didn't tell anything about the depth and intensity of their love for each other. Cole had not learned of her pregnancy until years later when she contacted him about Tom having fallen in with a gang of outlaws, while he was still a boy, really. Cole had rescued him, but Tom had broken the law even though he'd been little more than an accessory to the gang's activities, a horse holder. Despite those warrants for his arrest, Cole would not arrest him, and instead let him go to be with his mother in hopes that the law would overlook Tom's connection with the gang. But the law had not and had chased him and Anna into Canada, and they had become lost to Cole until now.

"I got to get on," Tom said. "I did what she asked, and now

it's finished."

He started to turn his horse away, but Cole took hold of its bridle. "I'd like us to work out the kinks," he insisted. Tom looked worn and hungry and his horse was lathered in spite of the cold. Cole appealed to his son's better sense. "Your horse could stand a blow and there's grain in that shed yonder and water in the tank."

Tom looked back over his shoulder, as if someone had been following him, but no one had been. Then when he turned back around again, his gaze ran over the place, then settled on Cole again. "I reckon just a few minutes, but then I got to get on."

Preacher Man had stopped several feet away, almost in a protective stance in case Cole had need of him. Charley had withdrawn his rifle altogether from the window and turned to stare up at Franzetta who'd come from the back bedroom, drawn by curiosity.

"Says he's John Henry's boy," Charley whispered. She bent to look out the window at Tom sitting the saddle horse. "He sure as heck is, you can see it," she commented.

Tom dismounted and walked his horse over to the water tank and busted the thin sheet of ice that had formed, then let his horse drink. Cole went and filled a feedbag with grain and handed it to Tom to put on the animal's head.

"I didn't come because I wanted anything from you," Tom said. "Just want you to know that."

Cole felt something ancient tear at his heart, something he could not explain to anyone but those who'd felt it, too—that thing called unsustainable grief. "Come, set a spell," Cole said. "Please tell me about your mother, what she died of, did she ever remarry . . . ?"

"That boy looks half starved," Franzetta said. "I'll fix him a plate."

"Help me with these crutches first so I can go out and

103

introduce myself."

"Why do you want to introduce yourself?" she asked.

"Just because," he said.

So she helped him get up and onto his crutches, and he went out to get a better look at this progeny of Cole's. He said as he stood there: "My wife's inside, fixing you a plate. My name's Charley Hood, in case you're wondering. I'm an associate of your pa."

Tom didn't offer to shake his hand but instead looked uncomfortable.

The three of them stood silently for a moment listening to the crunch of the horse eating grain.

Franzetta broke the spell when she came out with a plate of food—cured ham slices and pinto beans and biscuits, coffee, too.

"Here, you eat something," she said, and held forth the victuals.

"Thank you kindly," Tom said, and went and sat on the chopping block to eat, resting the plate on his knees as he drank some of the coffee.

"Looks starved as a wolf," Charley said. "You never told me you had a boy."

"It's a long story," Cole said.

Preacher Man stood silently, thinking that it was good that a man and his son were reunited, that seemed right.

Cole came and squatted beside Tom.

"How'd you find me?" he asked.

"She told me this is where you'd probably be."

Cole didn't remember talking to Anna about this place. He'd gotten it after he'd taken Tom back to live with her, following the death of her husband.

"I never would have thought it," Cole admitted.

"There toward her end days she talked a lot about you. She

heard about how you'd got this place. Don't ask me how. She said if I found you alive anywhere, it would probably be here at this place."

"There was every likelihood I might not have been here when you came. What if that had been the case, what would you have done?"

"I would have waited. She said wait out the winter, and if you hadn't come by the following spring, you were most likely dead."

Cole dropped his eyes to the ground between his boots. Anna had always had a certain gift about knowing things, even unspoken and unseen things. "What'd she die of?"

"Got a bloody cough. Doctor called it consumption. Gave no hope of her living through it. She didn't act scared of dying. Just asked me to take her home and come find you, and so that's what I did."

"You're welcome to stay here long as you want," Cole said. "Rightfully this place will fall to you anyhow, once I've passed."

Tom looked about, looked as far as he could see in every direction. Away off to the west and south he saw a faint jagged line of some mountains—must have been a hundred miles off. To the east and north lay mesas stretched out, black rock. The sun had broken through the gloomy sky and spread its light over everything, sparkling in the snow so that the snow looked like spilled sugar, as if you could scoop it up and put it in your coffee.

"It's a fair place," Tom said, then laid into a biscuit, the crumbs dribbling down his shirt front.

"I would have married her, just so you know," Cole said.

"She told me as much."

"I'm sorry for how things turned out."

"Don't be on my account."

"But I am."

Tom looked directly into his father's eyes, and it was a mite like looking at himself, those eyes. "I don't guess I'll be staying," he said. "It ain't my land."

"Law still hunting you?"

"I reckon they are. You ought to know the law don't quit."

"I maybe could help out with that."

"I sure don't see how."

"I'm friends with Judge Parker over in Fort Smith. I could write him a letter on your behalf."

"It won't do no good."

"How do you know it won't?"

Tom looked away, concentrated on the last of the beans on his plate. "I need to get my horse new shoes," he said. "Is there some place close around here?"

"There's Lusk, about ten miles' distance. Just a burg, but they got a blacksmith there I reckon could shoe your horse."

"Which way is it?"

"Tell you what. Why don't we take the wagon. You tie that spotted horse on back, and we'll ride over there together. Give us time to talk."

"I don't see's we got much to talk about."

"Maybe not, but it would be a great waste for you to come all this way and not get said what you want said, not ask questions you might want to ask. Me as well."

"If that's what you want."

"It is."

"Like to get started sooner rather than later."

"What's your great hurry?"

"I'm just restless is all . . . all these years of being on the dodge has made me restless."

"We'll leave now."

And so they did—headed for Lusk.

CHAPTER FIFTEEN

Two days after receiving the telegram, Birdy Peach and Slade Yellowbone stepped off the mud wagon.

"Well, if this still don't look like the devil's toilet," Slade said, looking around at the town of Buffalo Jump.

"Let's go find Constable Metz," the sheriff suggested.

Lazlo Metz wasn't a professional lawman even though his current job as a constable might mislead one into thinking so. He'd taken the job of constable because the town council, such as it was—a contingent of Cur Headly, who owned the hardware store, Juno Fly, and Emile Fritz—had practically begged him to.

"All right," he had said, completely unsure of what he was doing. "I'll do it."

There was a sigh of relief and the nickel badge was pinned on and an oath upon an old Bible was quickly sworn.

"Do you have a gun, Lazlo?" Juno Fry had asked.

"No, I'm a schoolteacher," Lazlo had said.

There were nervous smiles.

"But you need a gun if you are to maintain the law," Cur Headly had said.

Lazlo wasn't so sure about this last. First of all he'd been raised a Quaker and was firmly against any sort of violence or mayhem. He believed deeply in the goodness of man and the sanctity of life. "We don't have very much trouble that requires the use of a firearm," he had protested. "Just a few drunks who sometimes get into fights and have to sleep it off."

"Yes," Emile Fritz had conceded, "but do you remember the time when old Mister Harper murdered his wife and holed up in his house and wouldn't surrender and threatened to shoot anyone who tried to arrest him? You remember that, Lazlo?"

Lazlo had recalled the incident.

"And we had to send for Sheriff Birdy Peach and his deputy, Slade Yellowbone, and they come down here and how much of a gunfight it turned into before they burned the house down around him?"

"Yes."

"Well, that's why you should carry a gun, in case something terrible like that were to happen again."

Lazlo wondered if he could actually shoot someone if the circumstances were dire enough. He could still see the charred remains of old Mr. Harper when they dragged him from the ruins of his house, how awful and non-human he looked. Lazlo promised to get himself a gun, but he never did.

Then a few days back those outlaws had ridden in and robbed the bank and shot up the town, killing three people. *If only I would have listened and bought a gun,* Lazlo was thinking for the thousandth time, *I might have been able to stop those devils and saved Emile's and Juno's life as well as that of the Tolvard boy. Now look at what's happened.*

He paced and fretted while awaiting the arrival of Sheriff Birdy Peach, and then suddenly there the sheriff stood, along with that evil-looking deputy, Slade Yellowbone.

"Well, Constable," Birdy said, "we've come to find your killers and get back the bank money. What can you tell us, and which way did they go?"

Lazlo told them everything he knew about the robbery, and then about how he had been over at the infirmary helping Lila Patterson care for the sick and feeding soup to those who could not do it for themselves. He did not admit that one of his reasons for offering his assistance was because he was sweet on Lila, even though she was a married woman. It would not do to admit such a thing, but his heart burned brightly if unrequitedly for her.

"Feeding soup?" Slade said caustically.

"We do what we can for one another in Buffalo Jump," Lazlo replied.

"Seems to me you'd have done a lot more for one another by shooting down those dogs who robbed your bank and killed your townsfolk," Birdy said.

"You didn't get so much as a shot off?" Slade asked.

"No, sir."

"Why not?" Slade wondered.

Lazlo struggled to utter the truth. "I had no gun."

"No gun! What the hell sort of lawman are you?" Slade growled.

"A peaceful one."

Birdy snorted. So did Slade.

"Peaceful peace officer, well, now ain't that an interesting idea," Birdy said.

"Sort of like a three-legged race horse," Slade said.

"Or a real tall midget."

"Or a short beer."

They were having fun at his expense and Lazlo knew it, but he did not feel up to challenging them.

"You're lucky those miscreants didn't send you to perdition," Birdy said.

"I would have shot you for just being plain dumb," Slade said. "Laughed, and then shot you and gone about the whole country saying how I'd come up against an unarmed lawman."

This only made Lazlo feel even more terrible, made him want to run and hide and never show his face again.

"Well, we'll go over to the bank and see how much they

absconded with," Birdy said.

Lazlo remained still, like a scolded schoolboy. He no longer wanted anything to do with being the town constable. He wasn't even sure he wanted anything to do with remaining in Buffalo Jump, though the thought of moving away from Lila pained him. He watched the sheriff and his man cross the street and head for the bank.

Birdy and Slade soon learned that the amount of stolen money was over $15,000, nearly the entire sum of the bank's holdings except for the sacks of coins—silver dollars and liberty head dimes—and that the outlaws had fled west, and that a posse had gone after them but had returned empty-handed before dusk the same day.

"We best get in the wind," Birdy said, "if we have any hopes of finding those rascals and retrieving that money."

Once they had gotten fresh mounts and some supplies to sustain them for a few days—cured bacon, sugar, coffee, tobacco, and of course whiskey—they rode off in the direction they were told the outlaws had gone.

"We'll press them hard," Birdy said. "If they've got some wounded like Lazlo thought, they won't be able to move all that fast. And since it's been three days, they'll likely not fear anybody coming after them. They'll hole up somewheres, I do believe, and lay low while they lick their wounds. But we'll find them."

"If we're lucky, they'll still have all that stole money on them and won't get a chance to spend much of it."

"We'll make sure they never get to, either," Birdy said. "Fifteen thousand split two ways is a right smart day's wages."

"Plus whatever we can get for their horses and guns, and then the reward money on top of that," Slade said.

"And we'll come out looking like heroes. Guaranteed to get me elected to a second term. Why by the time I finish cleaning up this county, we'll be richer than a railroad baron, me and you, Slade. Hell, I might even run for governor."

"I don't know why everybody isn't a lawman," Slade said. "The pay's right smart if you know how to collect it."

"Me, either. But be glad they're not, or there wouldn't be no criminals and we'd be out of a job."

"Hell, one of us might have to take up the Owlhoot Trail and the other be the lawman just so we'd have some work."

"We'd have to flip a dollar for it."

Slade allowed himself a rare laugh.

"I do believe every man in this whole United States who has made himself a fortune, big or small, has done it illegal," Birdy said. "Big ranchers started out as rustlers, bankers and lawyers are nothing more than legal thieves, and so it goes. We're no different, you and me, Slade. And like them others, folks will look up to us and sing our praises, for the common man loves the successful one."

"They'll write dime novels about us," Slade predicted.

They soon enough found old blood sign, and later that day a camp with cold ashes. They followed horse tracks that turned north into some rough, beat-up country, scarred by arroyos and hidden little cañons. The next day, down through a sandy wash, they found more tracks and more blood sign.

"They might as well be leaving us notes," Birdy said.

"I can't wait to kill them peckerwoods," Slade said.

"We'll ask them to surrender, then kill 'em."

"I say we should do it the other way around," Slade said.

"Whatever works out best," Birdy said.

The second night they encamped under a railroad trestle. A bright full moon, like a newly minted silver dollar, rose above the trees, then teetered for a time upon a ridge. The land was empty, it seemed, except for the pair of them. Come first dawn they were back in the saddle, pressing on, Slade reading sign like it was a book. They only stopped for the horses to have a blow as they drank canteen water and ate beef jerky while in the saddle. The third night they made camp by a small pond of spring-fed water. The water was cold and sweet, and in the night Birdy said in a semi-drunken state after sharing yet another bottle of Old Tub, what he was going to do with some of the bank and reward money. He wanted to buy a cathouse. "Hell, I'll hire me all the best-looking wimmen and charge double the going rate."

"Wimmen," Slade said sourly.

"Sure, why not? What's the two things men will pay good money for even if it's their last dollar? Liquor and wimmen."

Slade snorted. He had become increasingly quiet, even more so when he was deep into his cups. For his thoughts kept wandering back to the mercantile clerk. In his silent reverie, Slade recalled a great uncle of his about whom it was said he had become a camp follower—a fancy cognomen for prostitute—during the Civil War. Uncle France had dressed as a woman and played the part of a woman to the men who came to visit him in his tent under the pretense of having their laundry done. It seemed at the time when Slade had first heard this strange and disturbing story that it simply could not be so. But nowadays, Slade had begun to wonder if maybe there wasn't something that ran in the family blood, maybe skipped a generation or two, and struck him. Maybe he was like his Uncle France, a fancy boy. It gave him the shudders to think so. *Wimmen,* he thought.

The night stars seemed so near they could just reach out and pick them like frozen fruit from a tree. Slade wondered what Jody was doing this night. In bed, alone? Something cold shuddered through him—like he'd swallowed a frozen star.

"Hell, maybe you'd need you an enforcer in that cathouse," he said to Birdy. "I'd admire some of that action myself."

It was a big fat lie of course, but Birdy didn't know that, and it was best to keep Birdy in the dark about what Slade had in mind once they caught and rubbed out the Sam Starr gang. How Birdy had talked about all that money split two ways. Well, why not just split one way? Wouldn't that last a man a lot longer than two ways?

"Pass that Old Tub," Birdy said, "and I'll think about making you my right-hand man."

Somewhere out in the far dark and lonely night a coyote yipped, and then another, and another, until there was a whole chorus of them. Slade wondered whatever had happened to Uncle France. Nobody in the family seemed to know. He never did come back from the war. Some figured him to have been killed, either by the enemy or his own kind—found out, perhaps, and murdered for his depravity. Uncle France wasn't very often spoken about, and never in the company of any of the Yellowbone womenfolk. It was always just whenever some of the Yellowbone men had gathered and shared a jug of mash liquor and got to talking about one thing or another. Mostly when Uncle France's name passed their lips, it was contained in such phrases as—"Can you believe it?"—or—"Thet boy was surely tetched in the head."

I am surely cursed, Slade told himself as he listened to Birdy's snores, to the coyotes' yips, to the silence of stars. He felt like killing somebody. Killing always seemed to help for some reason or other. Always made him feel like a true man and allayed his fears about the other thing.

Chapter Sixteen

They reached Lusk by sunset, Tom and John Henry Cole. It was still hard for Cole to believe that Tom had showed up. Even though he seemed more like a complete stranger, Tom was still his flesh and blood. He decided that no matter what, he was going to try and get to know this boy and do for him what he could, and not let him go again. Tom had an innocence about him, but he also had an edge to him as hard and sharp as a Barlow blade.

They talked little, however, each searching for words they could speak that might mean something to the other one. For Tom, finding his father again, a man his mother had talked much about in her last days, seemed surreal, like a dream he'd had so often about meeting up with this man once more, the man who once virtually saved his life before abandoning him. But now that he had found him again, it wasn't anything like a dream. John Henry Cole seemed too hardened and grizzled a man ever to have wooed and won his mother's love, Anna Rain who had been pretty and petite and of delicate sensibilities. And yet, she had allowed this man to get her pregnant, had been apparently abandoned by him, and so she had married Jimmy Wild Bird, a man approved by her father. She had told Tom how he had been taken from her at birth by his grandfather, and how great the shame had been over the pregnancy.

"The man who would have been your step-dad had he lived,

Jimmy Wild Bird, I was with him, you know, when he died," Cole said.

"My mother told me that. She said he knew about the two of you, but he never knew about me, never saw me. He didn't know I was called Red Snake . . . or what the men I was with did."

"No," said Cole, "he never did. And he was killed trying to capture Caddo Pierce, the man you were riding with in those days."

"My mother said Jimmy Wild Bird died of blood poisoning."

"That's right. It was either getting his arm cut off, or dying. He chose to die. He was a proud man. I liked him. Like they say, he was one to ride the river with. It was an honor for me, riding with him. He was a good man."

Tom held the reins threaded between his fingers as the little town of Lusk came into view, the first lights of evening shining from inside some of the establishments and homes. A collection of buildings scattered like seeds within a cup of land not unlike a buffalo wallow, the whole place seemed more accidental than planned. What caused such places to be birthed was anyone's guess. They simply were, and some survived the passage of time and fortune, and some did not. In the blue-black dusk a bawling rose and fell in a soulful sound that seemed to speak of great loneliness, as if the very land itself was crying out.

Cole had noticed a scar on Tom's face like a knife cut that had healed but had left a trough through the flesh above the left eye and curved slightly downward like the letter C.

"How'd you come by that?" he asked.

Without bothering to look at him, Tom said: "A Canucker. Me and him got into it more'n once. I guess he expected me to quit every time, but I wouldn't quit. I just would come back at him every time, and one day I came at him and finally beat him up, so that was the end of it."

Cole's smile was a bitter one—proud that his son had stood his ground, sad that he'd had to stand it at all.

"I guess you have a right to be bitter."

"It don't matter to me one way or the other. Where'd you say that smithy was?"

"Up ahead, there at the end of the street."

Tom passed through the center of the town and reined the mules over where a silent forge stood, and set the foot brake, then wrapped the reins around the handle. He and Cole climbed down.

A thick-set man lay snoring under a buffalo robe, his heavy boots poking out one end, his thicket of head hair out the other. He sounded like a busted steam pipe.

Cole tapped him on the soles of his boots until he stirred awake.

"Waugh!"

"Got a horse needs being shod," Cole said.

The man sat up, knuckled sleep from his eyes, and stared at the two of them in the soft buttery light of a bull's-eye lantern hanging from a nail driven into a thick support post. "Bring her around. I'll have to stoke up the forge. Need pay in advance."

"How much?" Cole asked.

"Four dollars all four shoes. Unless you need just one."

"All four will do."

"Come back in an hour and she'll be done."

"I'll wait," Cole said.

"I'd as soon walk around and see what's here," Tom remarked.

"Go ahead."

Cole watched him go off, swallowed up by the dark places. He sat while the smithy stoked the forge to life with bellows, coal oil, and matches. He built himself a shuck and smoked as he tried to piece together the events of the day, wondering what sort of luck or fate it was that Tom had come back into his life after all this time, and found himself nearly overwhelmed with happiness that Tom had. *Maybe I'm getting a second chance for a reason,* Cole thought as the smithy pried off the old shoes from the Appaloosa and filed the hoofs, preparing them for the new shoes. He took measurements and began to heat the new shoes in the forge. He was a stout man, as you'd have to be, his forearms knotted into hard muscles, his wrists and hands thick, strong as he plunged one shoe into the coals and heated it, then removed it when it got hot enough. He hammered it into shape before cooling it in bucket of cold water. Over and over again, working steadily, assuredly, his eye keen, his labor intent and sure as that of any craftsman. The hammer rang against the steel of shoe and anvil, rang sharply enough that Cole had to step away. The smithy's face was a sheen of sweat over soot, the sparks flying and the coals breathing like some fiery creature against the outer darkness.

Cole imagined a future with Tom, the two of them mending fences with each other, getting past the unfamiliarity of lapsed time. He allowed himself to imagine getting old and Tom marrying and settling into the house and babies coming who'd sit on his lap, and call him grandpa. He was letting his thoughts gallop away with him when shots rang out. Without knowing for certain, something told Cole that trouble had returned.

CHAPTER SEVENTEEN

One-Eye moaned and cursed his poor luck and said: "Can't one of you-all dig this damn' bullet outta my leg, or am I to suffer and bleed to death?"

Sam Starr looked askance at his wounded soldier. "Stop your god-damn' whining."

"Go to bloody hell!" One-Eye said through clenched teeth.

Black Bill was the handiest among them to patch up shot people. He'd been on burial detail during the war, but had watched a lot of those field surgeons cut and slice the wounded, had seen them saw off arms and legs and toss them into a pile. And sometimes they'd require him to hold a man down while they did their cutting and he'd watch them carefully, how they did it, dig out slugs and sew up wounds, how they'd wash the wounds with cleansing water and all the rest. "I'll give it a try," Black Bill said.

One-Eye looked at him skeptically. "You know what you're doing?"

"I don't have to do nothing you don't want me to do. Lay there and suffer and bleed to death, or wait for lead poisoning to set in and kill you."

A small fire flickered, the flames licking at the night. They had ridden their mounts hard and now they had to rest them. So far no posse had followed. They figured they were mostly in the clear.

Shorty had cooked up a pot of beans, and Atticus Creed

stood guard with his Winchester rifle.

"No, go ahead and cut it out of me," One-Eye pleaded.

"It's going to hurt like a sum-bitch," Black Bill said.

"Give me some more whiskey to drink."

"Sure."

Bill handed him the whiskey, and, as he was drinking it, Bill brought the barrel of his pistol down on hard on One-Eye's skull, knocking him cold as a metal doorknob. Atticus Creed thought he heard bone cracking.

"You killed that bastard," he said.

"Nah, he ain't killed. Look, he's still breathing."

"You might have scrambled his brains, though."

"Hell, he never did think right to begin with. Maybe I scrambled them to normal, you never know."

Atticus looked on with interest as Bill took out his pig-sticker and ran the blade through the fire.

"Why you doing that?"

"Heat kills the germs."

"Germs?"

Then Bill slit open One-Eye's bloody pant leg and cut away the knotted kerchief One-Eye had tied to stop the bleeding as much as possible. It was soaked and crusted with his blood. The wound hole was neat and round and wet-black, and when Bill dug into it with his knife, it looked like overripe fruit pulp. "It's in there deep," Bill said to no one in particular.

"Jesus, that looks like it hurts," Atticus said.

"That's why I cracked him over the skull."

He dug until he found the slug, then pried it free, and plopped it in his hand—a quarter ounce of lead. "Now I got to sew him up."

"With what?"

"I don't know." It was a conundrum with no needle or thread. Bill washed the bloody kerchief with canteen water and twisted the old blood from it, and washed it a little more, then packed it into the wound. "It'll have to do for now. We get somewheres I can buy a needle and thread, and I'll stitch him up, if he ain't died by then."

They ate the beans and rolled up in their bedrolls. One-Eye would wake, then fall back to sleep again, his head throbbing and leg aching. He suffered a vicious dream: being beaten by a mob over a pie he stole. They hit him over the head and broke his leg.

Come morning they were on the move again, headed for their hide-out that stood upon a long ridge that jutted southwestward, which they called the Devil's Den. They had built stone walls thirty inches thick, and it had twenty portholes instead of windows. It stood where No Man's Land played out and emptied into Texas or New Mexico, take your pick. Far as anybody knew, it had always been an outlaw hide-out of one sort or another. And it belonged to whichever gang took it over. Such hide-outs were few and far between on the otherwise flat and featureless Cherokee Outlet. But they existed, if you knew where to look for them. The gang was glad to return, rest up, lick their wounds, and also fornicate with the women they kept there, women who could sooth them, cook and clean and lay with them. Women they had brought from various watering holes and whiskey dens—down-trodden women to whom a place like the Devil's Den looked like heavenly refuge, women with dark pasts and little future. There were always women like that on the frontier. Women who'd come with adventure in their hearts—schoolteachers and seamstresses, and one even a former librarian from Indianapolis.

For such women, the frontier had proved unusually cruel. And while men were plentiful, most of them lived hand to mouth—cowpunchers and prospectors and even teamsters. The good, solid men were almost always already taken; the leavings were just that, leavings and poor prospects. A woman either cared for herself or was taken care of. Employment choices were few and poorly paid. Even a waitress job was hard to come by. So most of them ended up in houses of prostitution or as crib girls. After so many men, it hardly mattered who the next man was. A lot of them just gave up, drank mercury, and ended their young lives, and some of them retreated back home again—to Iowa and Ohio and Michigan, and found farm boys to marry them, never revealing their sullied pasts. For if a gal washes her body and hair and puts on a clean dress and acts demure, what farm boy could know of her past, except that which she might tell him?

An outlaw gang needed women and certain women needed an outlaw gang. Such were those waiting in Devil's Den: Josie Miller and Sue Elderberry and Flossie Jones. They were shared, and no one woman belonged to any one man, although Sam Starr as leader got first choice, and generally Josie was Sam's, her being the youngest and best-looking among them. She would lay with him until he tired of her, then let the others have their turn with her. Privately she quite liked the situation even though she preferred Black Bill among the gang, for he was the most rutting man she had ever encountered and always brought her to her own pleasure instead of just his own. But she knew that she could never let on to the others, Sam especially, that she favored Bill for fear that she would be sent away, back to the bagnios and cribs.

It would still be half a day's ride more to the cañon. Atticus Creed kept watching their back trail. He was the best of them when it came to shooting a Winchester. Shorty liked to tease Atticus by saying he'd come out of his ma carrying a Winchester. Atticus was by nature a serious man who did not take well to ribbing, that's why Shorty ribbed him so much—like a kid poking at a rattler till it coiled up to strike.

Shorty always knew when to quit—before Atticus got that look in his eyes. Sometimes Sam Starr would have to step in between them to get him to cool off and to get Shorty to lay off him. Everything was a game with Shorty. Maybe it was his short stature that made him feel as though he had to try and make things even between him and taller men. As far as a thinker, he was probably the best of them in the brains category. He'd even gone two years to college—the College of William and Mary in Virginia. He had thought of becoming a priest for a time but quickly realized that such a life didn't truly suit him. He loved too much the wine and women and knew that every warning about over-indulgence and fatal women was probably true, which made such things even more alluring. His real name was Julian Haysmith, but he hated that name. He hated the name Shorty, too, but couldn't do much about it.

Shorty and Sam Starr were the closest of the gang, having met and served time in the Detroit House of Corrections, where Judge Parker had sent Shorty for horse stealing. Sam was in for whiskey-peddling in the Nations. They had shared a cell, Sam saying that winter: "Jeez Christ, you ever been so cold in your life, Shorty?"

"One time in Alaska it was colder'n this."

"Alaska? What the hell were you doing way up there?"

"Searching for gold, same as everybody else."

"You find any?"

"Hell no. All gone, time I got there, except for the big outfits."

"I hear a fellow can get et by a bear up there, they're so damn' big and plentiful. Hear you have to fight them for the fish."

"That's true," Shorty said. "Ten feet tall at least and around every bend."

"I can't wait to get out of this place. I never seen nothing like it. How many horses did you steal, anyway?"

"Almost forty . . . me and this other fellow named One-Eye. Stole 'em off some Indians over in the Nations, Cherokees they was, according to court records."

"The horses were Cherokee, or was it the Indians you stole 'em off of?"

That's what Shorty had liked about Sam Starr, his sense of humor and quick wit. They got along fine, and when Shorty got out, he waited for Sam Starr and together they headed to the Cherokee Outlet on some horses Shorty had stolen.

"I guess you didn't learn a god-damn' thing, did you, Shorty?"

"No, I reckon not. It was either steal these nags or walk."

They had sold the horses on a fake bill of sale when they hit the town of Tulsa, and then Shorty stole two more from the same man that very night, and they rode off on them. They had robbed a fellow in Lawton of $27 and a brass watch. They had broken into a home in Guymon and held a man at gunpoint while they took turns raping his wife, then shot them both deader than ducks and carried off the silverware and whatever money they found plus a cuckoo clock. One night, both of them drunk, they had taken pot shots at the little red bird every time it popped out of the clock until they finally had killed it, the clock shot all to pieces.

"They ain't no turning back now," Shorty had said in a melancholy mood once the liquor had begun to wear off.

"Never was no turning back for me once I left my ma's cunny," Sam had replied from the shadows of their little camp. "They will have to shoot me dead before I'd ever go back to any sort of jail."

"And I reckon they *will* shoot you dead, they ever catch up to us for what we done to them people. Shoot you and me both. There isn't one man who'd sit on the jury would find us innocent or show any sort of mercy."

123

"Well, fare-thee-well and hallelujah, I say," Sam had howled, and had done a little jig. Shorty admired him because he didn't seem to fear a thing, including dying. Shorty had determined then and there to stick very close to Sam Starr.

Eventually it was Shorty who got One-Eye to join them. One-Eye Peck was an all-around kind of thief who would steal anything of value and do anything that would earn him a dollar. He didn't care what the crime was and seemed to have no conscience about his acts. He had been a Mormon once and part of the militia that had attacked the Fancher-Baker party that would later be known as the Mountain Meadows Massacre. It was where, in fact, he'd lost an eye, during that fight, or slaughter, whichever you might want to call it, a bullet fragment from one of his own militiamen clipping his right eye and blinding it. He had fallen wounded and laid in the grass as the killings went on. He was half sickened by what took place and rode away from there, never again to return to Utah or the Mormon Church. He'd come to believe that all religion was bad and no good ever came from it.

The frontier proved nearly as hard for a one-eyed man to make a living in as it did for a woman. He had come to learn this while working as a bouncer in a Colorado bordello in Leadville. He had gotten to know the working girls quite well, and related to their plight, and they in turn had taken him into their fold like a wounded bird. He had fallen in love with one called Maggie, and they had made plans to marry. But then Maggie had caught the pox and slowly died from it, and One-Eye had gone on his way, back out into the world of horse thieves, cutthroats, murderers, and blackguards. He'd met Shorty in the Nations, and they had teamed up to steal horses from Indians because Indians generally kept the best stock. After Shorty got arrested and sent to the Detroit House of Correction, One-Eye had cleared out of the Nations for a time and headed to Texas.

He had written Shorty, telling him that he was going to try his hand in Mobeetie, and if that didn't pan out, he might head to Amarillo, and if ever Shorty got out and needed a partner, to get hold of him in one of those three places General Delivery. That's what Shorty did, he and Sam Starr and by that time Atticus Creed and Black Bill, also.

Pat Gunnerson became the other member of their gang—a mean hardcase from New Mexico where he'd gunned down at least three lawmen in a bad fight in Las Vegas. He and Sam Starr were old acquaintances, Sam Starr saying to the other boys: "He's a real mean peckerwood you'd best be careful around, for he won't hesitate to shoot you in the back. But he's a real fighter, and, if we get into it with a bunch of lawdogs, you can count on Gunnerson to stand and fight."

After Gunnerson came on board, the entire lot of them felt uneasy about him, even when they were holed up in the Devil's Den. He went about talking to himself, almost always drunk and leering at the women. He was rough with them, and Sam Starr had to warn him not to be.

"You can get what you want off them, just don't be so damn' rough. They'll give it to you."

Gunnerson was always reading the pocket Bible he had and spouting off about what he read in it. "Iffen any man or any woman fornicates with a animal, both the human and the animal ought to be killed . . . it says that here in the book of Leviticus." Reading such things would often cause him to giggle. "Any you boys had sex with a animal . . . if so, I'll have to burn you up?"

They stayed shy of Gunnerson. And it was sweet relief when he had gotten gunned down in Buffalo Jump. There were no tears or sad feelings felt among them, simply good riddance all around.

By early afternoon they rode into the cañon, and up it to the Devil's Den. The three women seemed eager for their return, and that night everyone feasted on good cooked food and Shorty got out his fiddle and set to playing and the others danced a reel, and everybody got good and drunk. And before midnight fell and the full moon rose, fornication was well at hand and nobody worried about any damned posse finding them.

But no more than a half day's ride behind were two men who aimed to track them down, kill them, and take the money and every last thing they had, including their bad reputations.

CHAPTER EIGHTEEN

The man had been drinking but was not yet drunk, simply belligerent and on the prod. He'd had a fight with his wife, which was not unusual for the two of them. Both were boozers and both had long suffered the company of the other. The wife—Vineta Sorghum Blue—had spent half her forty years fighting with one man or another over one thing or another. She'd worked as a ranch cook for several of those troubled years before T. Bone Blue came along, constantly either rebuffing the advances of cowpunchers or accepting them. She had become known as an easy mark among the boys, and maybe she was and would be the first to admit it, but she liked to believe that she wasn't easy with every last one of those yahoos. That she had a modicum of discretion, though after so many men the line of reasoning became blurred.

It was while a ranch cook that she'd met T. Bone Blue, an oft-times drifter and saddle tramp who took work only when he had to. T. Bone Blue might not have a thin dime in his pocket and yet he acted as if the world was his oyster to eat whenever he wanted to. He was also a ladies' man and liked to believe he could charm a snake out of its skin. He'd left a trail of wounded hearts, and whenever the occasion arose he not only stole their hearts, but their savings as well.

T. Bone Blue was wanted in several states and territories for being a bunko artist and a grifter, an alienator of affections and absconder. He always tried to keep one jump ahead of the law and thus far had been successful, using various aliases as he went. Until he met Vineta Sorghum, her unmarried name, as she put it. Vineta had big blue eyes and a rosy glow of a complexion, like a peach freshly rained upon and a sweet little bow of a mouth. She worked hard at keeping her weight down, and of course the opium that she smoked helped that particular cause.

She was sassy and knew how to lure any man alive—like fishing with real good bait, as she'd brag to some of her girlfriends. "It's easy, if you know which bait to use for which kind of fish you're after."

They had tittered with admiration.

Some might say that by the time they met, Vineta was the female version of T. Bone. She'd made suckers out of a lot of men—some of them deservedly so, and others not so much. Among other past occupations she'd been a dance-hall girl who sang for drinks and let the boys have a feel as a method of advertising the goods.

T. Bone met her in Big Jack Jones's Black Cat Emporium where she was currently plying her various talents. Big Jack got fifty percent of her earnings and an occasional roll in the hay whenever he required it.

Vineta and T. Bone were like a lit match dropped in spilt whiskey. Their senses just seemed to go up in flames, as did their passion for each other. They fornicated themselves nearly to death that first night and got married in the morning by a hung-over preacher.

Things between them went fine for about two days. Then they had their first big fight. And over the intervening weeks and months they seemed to fight constantly when they weren't fornicating. It was all the time, fight or fornicate, nothing in between. A lot of the fights came about over T. Bone's jealousy of Vineta's current profession.

"I hate you sleeping with those other men."

"Then you best get a job to support us."

"Job! I ain't no sort of working man. I make my living by my wits. My hand don't fit no broom handle ever made, nor no spade or hammer handle, either. It don't fit no plow or can of peaches off a shelf to sell to some rat-faced old crone."

"Your wits sure as hell ain't paying the rent or putting no food on the table."

She'd slap her rump and say: "But this here is and it's only one way to use it and seems to me you're getting it free, so I don't know what they hell those wits of yours are thinking."

Their arguments would escalate because neither could let it rest. They were like dogs fighting over a bone, too much pride or too little sense. At first it was only shouting, but soon it got physical between them. He'd slap her and she'd slap him back. He knocked her cold one time, but then felt sorry immediately and treated her like a princess for nearly a week. Until she tied him to the bed one night when he was sleeping, woke him with a bucket of water, and whacked him over and over with a broom handle.

"That's for knocking me out, you son-of-a-bitch."

It was two weeks till he could move without pain.

"I ought to kill you, woman."

"Maybe I'll kill you first!"

But sometimes such anger turned to passion, and when it did, it caused a healing of body and soul that was nearly miraculous and became the thing that bound them so tightly together. T. Bone Blue learned that when he got mad enough, he should leave the house before any hitting started. He sure enough did not want to wake up again tied to the bed and get beat by a broom handle, or possibly worse, because Vineta threatened that next time she'd take his own razor and cut off something near and dear to him. So lately, when things got heated, he'd leave the house and go to a saloon and drink until his anger subsided. But sometimes that took a while.

When Tom had left John Henry Cole, he'd walked up the street and quickly became distracted by the sound of a piano being played loudly—a gay, happy sound—and he figured he could use a little happiness right about then, so he sauntered into the place. It was a long, narrow room, like so many of them were, the walls so close together you had to be careful not to bump into somebody. It was mostly a place for locals who were not overly friendly by nature to strangers.

The professor and the piano sat right inside the door up against the wall that faced the street. He was a short stubby fellow under a bowler hat and wore his sleeves rolled up. His stubby fingers flew over the keys. Early in the evening he played fast, but as the evening wore on, he played slower and slower, knowing that the boys would become melancholy and drink more to forget their melancholy. Such was the way of lonesome and often lost men.

Tom squeezed past two or three fellows standing along the bar. Others sat at tables, playing stud poker. The air was hazed with blue smoke from cigars and cigarettes. Tom found a spot along the bar and ordered a beer. He'd never felt so much like a man as he did in that moment, drinking in a saloon among men, thinking: *Hell, I might even come to like this life.* He had about two sips of beer when T. Bone Blue bumped his elbow while telling a joke to some arm-bender standing next to him. T. Bone was expressive with his hands and one of them flew back and knocked Tom's arm as he was lifting his beer, causing it to spill all over the front of his shirt.

It might have been all right if T. Bone had turned to apologize. But he didn't. He just went on telling his damned stupid joke. Tom poked him in the back, hard.

T. Bone turned around and glared at him. "What the fuck

you want, Injun Joe?"

"You spilled my beer."

T. Bone looked him up and down and said—"Eat shit!"—and turned back to the fellow he was telling the joke to. That's when Tom shoved hard so that he crashed into the fellow he'd been telling the joke to and the fellow shoved T. Bone back into Tom just as hard. Tom called him a son-of-a-bitch and ordered him to apologize. That's all it took to push T. Bone over the edge of his earlier rage with Vineta.

Other's scrambled out of the way. Most of them knew T. Bone Blue, knew he could be a bad one when he chose to be, knew about him and his wife, how they were all the time fighting, and T. Bone walking around like misery itself just looking for a dog to kick. They didn't know this young man or what he was capable of, so they scattered like dog-chased quail.

T. Bone reached for his pistol—a belly gun stuck down in the waistband of his trousers. Only when he did, Tom clamped down on his wrist with an iron grip, keeping him from drawing the piece out fully and at the same time he drew his own revolver and fired once into the middle button of T. Bone's shirt.

"Ooff!" T. Bone sat straight down, grabbing his middle.

Tom stepped back, the barrel of his pistol leaking smoke, the gunshot so loud it brought complete silence from those who remained. The professor had taken refuge out on the street along with some others. The poker players had dropped under their table, scattering chips and coins.

"You shot me . . . ," T. Bone muttered in disbelief.

"You were going to shoot me."

"But you god damned shot me. . . ."

"I wished you hadn't made it come to this."

Along with others who'd heard the shot, John Henry Cole had come running instinctively at the sound, his first thought being: *Oh, no, somebody's killed my boy.* But it was Tom standing there, holding a smoking gun and not some other way around. Cole quickly stepped forth. He looked at the man sitting down, bleeding, and when he spoke Tom's name, Tom looked at him with a stranger's eyes.

"What happened, Son?"

It took a second more for recognition. "He tried to shoot me."

T. Bone leaned over on one elbow, still holding himself.

"Somebody get this fellow a doctor!" Cole ordered. One of the poker players headed outside.

"It's OK, Tom, it's OK, leave off now."

Tom seemed to come to cognizance then as to who he was and who John Henry Cole was, and the situation. He looked down at T. Bone, at the blood dribbling through his fingers, the twisted face of pain. He holstered his gun then, and Cole led him outside where light and shadows played between the open businesses and the closed ones. Figures of men moved in and out of the light. Word spread quickly that someone had shot T. Bone Blue. Somebody went to T. Bone's house and rapped furiously on the door—the knocking was not so much out of concern for either T. Bone or Vineta as out of some perverse satisfaction at being the fellow who carried the news to her that someone had finally shot that son-of-a-bitch husband of hers.

Vineta answered dressed in a silk wrapper.

"Come on in," she said, thinking the man was a customer.

He hesitated, caught a bit off guard by the invitation. Then when he realized the opportunity in it, he stepped inside and closed the door.

It was only later, when he paid her the money, that he told her about T. Bone's getting shot. "Your man's been gunned down," he said.

She had been drinking hard ever since T. Bone had stormed out earlier, and even before that, so such news befuddled her.

She laughed, and said: "To hell you say."

"No, ma'am, some feller shot him over in the saloon."

She blinked twice. "You mean you come here to tell me that and instead bought yourself a poke offen me?"

"Afraid it kind of seems so," he said. "Sorry."

She threw a china cup at his head as he was fleeing, then promptly passed out on the bed.

Meanwhile, at the saloon, bleeding on the dirty floor of spilled beer, tobacco spit, and shredded cigar butts, T. Bone had set to crying: "Where's my Vineta, where's my love?"

Cole said to Tom: "We'll wait till the marshal gets here and explain it. Pure case of self-defense."

The town marshal did come, a man named R.T. Dickens, and heard the tale from Tom and from others who'd seen it and those who claimed they had—for nobody much cared for that loudmouth T. Bone Blue, especially the way he sometimes treated the best whore in town—and the marshal said: "Where you boys from?" Cole told him, and the marshal mused for a moment, then said: "I know the place you mean. Wondered who owned it. All I ever saw around there was a crazy old Mexican in a frayed sombrero."

"Yes, sir," Cole said.

"You boys best get out of town and save me the paperwork. I'm late for supper as it is."

"No charges, then?" Cole asked.

The marshal looked at him and replied: "What'd I just say?"

Cole and Tom left.

"We're wise to accept his advise," Cole remarked. "Climb up. I'll drive back."

"Not before I get my horse," Tom said.

They stopped by the blacksmith's to get Tom's freshly shod horse and the smithy said: "You-all know what that shooting was about?"

"No," Cole said. "We heard it, too."

Then they drove away in Preacher Man's wagon with Tom's horse tied on back.

"There's a few things I need to teach you before you go off into the world," Cole said to Tom as they headed back to the cabin. "About shooting men, and such."

CHAPTER NINETEEN

"My ass hurts like a sum-bitch," Slade Yellowstone said.

He and Birdy Peach had stayed hard on the trail of the outlaws, driven by the smell of some easy money. They halted, not knowing they were less than an hour from the cañon and Devil's Den. Slade had to walk around, straddle-legged, because of the ache in his groin. Despite the pillow he sat on, the hard chase had pounded an ache into him where the bullet had gone through. *Pain like that you never get rid of,* he thought. He'd have it till the day he died. He swallowed a handful of cocaine pills with a couple of swallows from a bottle of Old Tub he kept in his saddlebags.

Birdy squatted in the sand of a dry wash, reading horse tracks.

"We're close," he said. "These tracks is fresh." There were also horse droppings, lots of them, and these Birdy smelled to confirm his suspicions they were closing the gap.

Slade walked about in circles trying to get the blood circulating through him so the pills and whiskey would take quicker effect. "Feels like I got to take a piss, but if I do, it'll be like pissing fire," he said.

Slade Yellowbone was perhaps the most dangerous man Birdy had ever known, but looking at him now, hobbling about and complaining like a whipped child made Birdy want to put a slug in him. *No, not yet,* he told himself. *Wait till after we get that stole bank and reward money. Just have to say ol' Slade got killed in the gunfight . . . died a brave man . . . and give him a cheap funeral.*

135

"Let me know when you're good to ride again," he said over his shoulder to Slade who was holding himself as he hobbled about.

Slade was thinking: *I'm going to kill you dead, Birdy Peach, wunst we get that money. You and them outlaws will dance together in hell. Ain't no way I'm gonna split that much money, not even with the devil hisself. Oh, you dumb bastard sum-bitch.*

The sun was already leaning toward the western horizon, the air still cold and everything dead-looking. Away off Birdy saw a jack rabbit running ahead of a coyote both of them going fast. *Life and death,* Birdy thought, *some do the chasing and others get chased.* "I 'spect we'll run them to ground by dark fall," Birdy opined. *And come the morrow I'm going to be one rich sum-bitch.*

Twenty minutes passed, and Slade could feel the pain draining out of him at the same time a cloud of euphoria overtook his senses. It was sort of like being drunk, he thought, only better. "I'm set. Let's go get them sum-bitches."

They mounted up, and rode along the wash and came out where the tracks of the gang tore up the side of the bank, and crossed a plain of alkali that lay white and nearly flat like a fresh-washed bed sheet.

Beyond the plain the landscape turned rocky and rose to a black mesa, and barely visible from where they sat were the rock walls of Devil's Den. Both men sat their horses at the edge of the alkali flat.

"Yonder they be," Birdy Peach said, pointing a gloved finger. "It's as far as you can go and still reside in the Nations. End of the line."

"We could be riding straight into a deathtrap," Slade said.

"Not if we do it right."

"What's the right way of doing it, Peach, other'n just riding in there?"

"We wait till dark and go the last bit on foot."

"It looks a long ways up in there to go in on foot."

"Horses would make too much noise."

"I don't know."

"You want that god-damn' money or not? Ain't nobody just going to hand it to us."

Slade stood in the stirrups to relieve the pressure on his groin, and when he did the red pillow with *HOME SWEET HOME* stitched on it fell to the ground and he failed to notice because the cocaine pills and whiskey had swarmed into his mind like a horde of bees whose every sting brought a new numbing to his thoughts.

"We'll cross this plain and wait there below the place," Birdy said, and spurred his mount forward, and Slade followed suit, thus leaving the red pillow in their wake. As evening set, a full moon rose above the rimrock and seemed to balance itself there for a time. It appeared more yellow than white because it was a blue moon—the sort that came twice in a month, and perhaps an omen of some sorts.

"The moon will give us light to see by, a good omen," Birdy said. "We'll leave our mounts here."

They hobbled their horses, then jerked their Winchesters free of their saddle scabbards, and filled their pockets full of extra shells. Each was also armed with a number of revolvers.

"Take off your spurs, too," Birdy ordered, "lest we sound like whores with loose change in our purses."

"I got these spurs down in Mexico," Slade said. "Custom made." The spurs were nickel-plated and had large rowels. Slade always went in for the fancy.

Up the rocky incline they started.

"I bet they're up there right now, sleeping like babies," Birdy said.

"Maybe we best just stop talking," Slade whispered.

So they fell silent as two nuns in church and picked their way up the rise, trying their best to be stealthy.

Sam Starr was putting it hard to Josie Miller. Of course, he had to share her with the others, but so long as he was first, he didn't care all that much. She was, after all, simply something to pleasure himself with.

Atticus Creed kept guard outside one of the walls where the air was fresh and without the musky scent of the sweat of sex, without the groaning and carrying-on of what took place inside. He'd let the others have their pleasure, but for himself he wasn't as keen on lying with the women of Devil's Den. He had a sweetheart back in Fort Smith that he was most keen on and felt as if he must remain true to her in spite of his outlaw ways. He believed that to sin against her was the same as to sin against God, who he believed guided him, guided them all, guided every man, woman, and child on earth and every living thing.

Atticus did not speak openly about his beliefs and held them very privately. He thought Pat Gunnerson was a fool for spouting things from the Bible. A fool and a false prophet for reading the things he did aloud, such as men having sex with animals. Atticus knew he shouldn't be glad that Pat had bought it in Buffalo Jump, but if there was ever a man who deserved killing it was Pat Gunnerson. Atticus himself had been raised Catholic and often wished he'd stayed on the straight and narrow instead of falling in with Sam Starr. Inez Bouchant was his sweetheart back in Fort Smith and he wore a silver St. Christopher medal around his neck that she'd given him. He carried an old tintype of her—a round-faced girl whose mouth held back a smile, whose dark eyes did not flinch at the camera's lens. Atticus felt much in love every time he looked at her. He had wanted a thousand times to go and be with her again. But as a wanted man he knew that, if he were to be arrested, he would go before

Judge Parker's Western District court and most likely be hanged. The thought of having Inez Bouchant see him being hanged was to Atticus worse than the hanging itself would have been.

No, let the others consort with whores, he would not. So, instead, he stood guard in the moonlit night, a cup of whiskey-laced coffee near at hand. It's all a man needed, just some coffee and a good rifle. He could hear them carrying on inside, Sam Starr and Black Bill—Shorty sawing on his fiddle—dancing, laughing, fornicating, all liquored up and full of themselves. One-Eye was complaining about his wound. Well, let them be. It had been a long ride from Buffalo Jump and he was as weary as he'd ever been.

Sometime in the night sleep took them all—whore and outlaw alike, for they were merely human.

Atticus's eyes, too, slowly drooped as he leaned against the outer wall, his Winchester cradled in his arms, his cup of whiskied coffee drunk down to the dregs. His head slumped. He did not notice the shadows of two stalking men go past his position, heading for the door. Nor did the stalking men notice Atticus Creed as they passed by where he dozed.

In a whisper Birdy said: "Inside is our game."

And like that, out of old habit more than anything, Slade levered a shell into the chamber of his Winchester, and the sound it made immediately alerted Atticus from his drowse. He blinked twice, looking about, and saw the two bent figures moving past him and closing in on the entrance.

He swung his rifle about and took aim and fired. Flame spit from his rifle barrel and his shot took down one of the figures.

Birdy felt the stinging punch of Atticus's bullet as it shattered his knee, felt himself falling, face into ground, his entire leg aflame. Slade wheeled about at the sound of the gunshot and fired his own rifle where he thought the shot had come from. The two shots ripped the still evening apart.

Inside, Sam Starr jumped up from the bed naked as the day he was delivered into the world and grabbed his pistols and ran out, firing them both, as did Black Bill who had bedded not one but both the other women in the encampment.

Suddenly the night was ablaze with gunfire from every direction with Birdy and Slade caught in a murderous crossfire. Like giant fireflies, yellow sparks of light danced in the darkness.

Birdy was screaming and shooting his rifle as fast as he could, jacking shell after shell in his Winchester, and Slade doing the same.

Shorty had also come alert and grabbed his pistol and commenced to make mayhem even though no one was exactly sure who or what the trouble was, just that it was trouble, and he figured the lawdogs had caught up with them. One-Eye got his right ear shot off by a stray bullet. Slade took a round through the elbow, paralyzing his left arm to his shoulder. His Winchester fell uselessly from his hands and clattered to the rocky ground.

Atticus Creed was hit by a chip of bullet striking rock that cut his face open as neatly as if it had been swiped by a straight razor.

Then Birdy got hit again, taking a slug in the belly, and he groaned and cried out even louder than before. "Holy Jesus! I'm shot clean through, Slade, those god-damn' sons-a-bitches!"

Slade without his Winchester jerked one of his revolvers and emptied it at Sam Starr, but Black Bill had taken careful aim and put a round through Slade's ribs and knocked him down. Sam Starr accidentally shot the toe off One-Eye's foot on the same leg in which he'd been shot during the bank hold-up. *They're shooting me to pieces!* One-Eye's mind screamed. The pain was maddening and caused him to try all the harder to get into the fight.

With both Birdy and Slade on the ground, they were like a pair of snakes that'd been run over by a wagon wheel, writhing in great pain but still dangerous. The gang poured lead into them in a murderous fire, and Slade Yellowbone and Birdy Peach felt every one of the slugs that ripped them to pieces, every slug but the last ones.

The firing did not cease until guns were empty and the shooters saw that nobody was any longer firing back.

Sam Starr shouted: "You women get some lanterns out here and let's have a look at these sons-a-bitches!"

Flames trapped in glass chimneys were brought forth, and held close to the anguished dead faces of the lawmen. Hands rifled through bloody clothing until badges were produced, and blood-soaked dodgers.

"Just like I thought they was," Sam Starr said. "God damn' dirty lawdogs."

Black Bill aimed his cocked pistol and fired his last round into the head of Slade Yellowbone, shattering his skull. Everybody jumped at the unexpectedness of the *coup de grâce*.

"Piss pots," Bill said, then spat on the corpses.

"They keep sending these bastards after us and we keep right on killing them. When're they going to quit?" It was an open question from Sam Starr.

One-Eye was yelping like a scalded dog from his wounds. "I'm shot to hell."

Atticus Creed stood quietly reloading his Winchester even though his face was bleeding. He seemed not to notice.

The women stripped the lawmen of their clothing and boots, wallets, a silver ring off the pinky finger of Birdy Peach, the one that his mother had given him years before. They took their guns as well. Birdy had three pistols on his person besides the Winchester rifle, and Slade had five. The bodies were riddled black from the bullets. The final fusillade had blown part of Birdy's jaw away as well. Several teeth were exposed, and Black Bill took his pig sticker and pried out one of Birdy's teeth that had a gold filling.

"They must have horses they left somewhere," Sam Starr said. "Why don't you go find 'em," he ordered Atticus.

Atticus turned without a word and went down the incline and soon enough found the two mounts and pack horse, and brought them back, thus adding to the largess.

"I guess they never expected this, those lawdogs didn't," Sam Starr said, passing around the whiskey they found in the lawmen's saddlebags.

Bill did his best at patching up One-Eye again, though the man was bleeding in so many places that Bill didn't know quite where to start first. He asked One-Eye: "You hear out of that ear?"

" 'Course I can!" shouted One-Eye.

"Well, you ain't got nothing left but a hole is why I was wondering."

One-Eye felt of the spot and found his external ear gone.

"I'll have to cauterize that toe stub, too."

"Don't hit me on the god-damn' head no more, just pass me some of that bug juice . . . enough till I get cross-eyed."

"How'll I know when that is, since you only got one damn' eye to begin with?"

"I'll laze over toward the middle."

There was plenty of whiskey for drinking pleasure and for medicinal purposes. And before anyone knew it, Shorty had whipped out his fiddle again and started playing a reel, and everybody, including One-Eye, got stinking drunk. Pretty soon there was fornicating as well in order to take the edge off their nerves.

"Only one way a man can relax," Sam said, "is plenty of whiskey and women."

The females obliged because for them there was something erotic they found in the violence of men, rough, wanting men who'd let blood and cursed and took what they wanted and were willing to die for their way of life. It was a powerful feeling.

Come sunrise, the naked white bodies of Birdy Peach and Slade Yellowbone still lay where they'd fallen, their blood soaked into the sand, and a wheel of buzzards high overhead in the pale blue sky had somehow got word there were bones that needed picking.

Sam Starr was the first to emerge from inside, stretching and feeling drained. He wore only his trousers and scratched at himself as he looked at the bodies and wrinkled his nose, for already they were starting to stink.

Atticus sat a ways off under a blanket, his hat lowered over his eyes, his Winchester cradled in his arms as usual. He only half drowsed so he opened his eyes at Sam's approach, and watched him carefully to see what he might do.

Sam undid himself and urinated on the dead men, saying the while: "That's what I think about lawdogs." Then, when finished, he said to Atticus: "Rope them by the heels and drag them off this promontory and leave them on the alkali plain for the buzzards and coyotes to have at."

Atticus rose and went and saddled a horse and did as instructed, but without joy or pleasure. These were, after all, still human beings and it seemed somehow wrong for one man to treat another as less so.

A cold wind rippled across the plain as though an omen that could not be deciphered as Atticus dragged the bodies to the alkali flats and unroped them. He offered up a silent prayer for their souls, if they had any. Then turned and rode back up the slope, and had his breakfast.

Chapter Twenty

Old Pablo came by on what most would call a two-bit horse with a ten-cent saddle. The horse was one he'd found wandering and half starved. It must have run off from some place was all he could figure. He'd fed and nursed it back to health. He'd rubbed liniment on its sore legs every morning and spoke to it in Spanish. And when it got filled out and didn't limp, he cinched an old McClellan saddle on it—one he'd also found one day while out looking for cow skulls. He'd found it in a dry wash. Not far away from the saddle lay the bones of a human, ribs and a skull and some long bones, too. Some poor soul no doubt had gotten lost on the featureless plains.

Old Pablo had thus far found only one saddle and one horse and a rusted Barlow knife in his wanderings. He hoped someday to find hidden treasure maybe, from outlaws that sought refuge in the Outlet. He'd heard rumors that a lot of stolen money was buried in haste.

He had eyes as dark as shoe buttons and leathery skin. He had no idea how old he was. And in spite of his historic past, he had mellowed with age now so that he did not want to kill any more people if it could be helped. Years and years ago, when he was a young man, he had been a border bandit and a lover of *señoritas* and *gringas.* He still carried on his person a tintype in a small metal frame of himself taken in a Chihuahua photography studio that showed him dressed in a fine straw sombrero, a silk jacket heavily embroidered with gold threads, and holding a brace of pistols. He thought he looked very cocky.

He recalled the day he had the photograph taken. It was a good day and he had had plenty of money, if illegally gained, and several girlfriends. It was the sweetest of times. Often he would take out the photograph and look at it for hours in his loneliest moments and wonder where and how the years between that young man in the tintype and what he saw in the mirror as he shaved in the mornings had gone so quickly.

Now even his own bones cursed him every morning when he arose from bed, and he was bedeviled by various ailments that would suddenly spring upon him like bandits, hiding in the brush of his life. His stomach would ache and go sour one day, and the next his eyes burned, and it was sometimes difficult to make water and he had to stand a long time trying to dribble what was causing his bladder to ache. Every day was a curse upon him and every night in his dreams it seemed as though he died again and again only to awaken dozens of times and wonder if he was yet alive or had died. His only joy, it seemed, was talking to his horse, or when John Henry Cole would come and stay at his cabin and he could visit with him, and they would tell each other stories about their lives.

"You know, I was once a very bad *hombre*," he had told Cole after they'd become friends and he knew he could trust the *gringo*.

"I've no doubt," Cole had replied.

"How do you know I'm not just making things up?" Old Pablo had said.

"You don't strike me as a man who would make things up. You strike more me like a man who needs to confess and be forgiven."

Pablo had smiled at Cole's wisdom.

"Maybe so."

"I'm not a priest," Cole had told him.

"I've made my peace with Him," Old Pablo had said, pointing a gnarled forefinger skyward.

"I don't think He'll judge us on what we were so much as what we are at the hour of our death. You want another drink of this bug juice?"

Of course Old Pablo had. He enjoyed drinking whiskey with John Henry Cole and was sorely disappointed when Cole had told him he had given up drinking. But Cole always kept a bottle on hand for Old Pablo, knowing that the old bandit could hardly afford liquor or much else—that he subsisted on shot rabbits and prairie dogs and occasionally a coyote. Cole would always lay in a supply of groceries for the old man whenever he'd come to the cabin. He truly liked Old Pablo as much as he'd ever liked any man. And Old Pablo saw a lot of himself in his *gringo* friend.

"I bet you have done some pretty bad things in your life, also," Old Pablo had hinted occasionally.

"I think anyone who lives to become a man has done bad things," Cole had replied. "I don't know how you couldn't."

"The devil is always trying to get us, eh?"

"I reckon you could look at it that way."

"You know that chimney isn't too straight," Old Pablo noticed when they had worked together on building the cabin—Old Pablo being a fair hand with a hammer and a level.

Cole had nodded. The chimney did not look very straight.

Together they got a respectable cabin built, and then sat around for three days admiring their work, Old Pablo drinking Cole's whiskey even though he preferred tequila, and Cole drinking black Arbuckle's and smoking cigarettes.

"How'd you ever end up way up here in this county?" Cole had asked him during those three days.

Old Pablo had shook his head and said simply: "I do not rightfully know. I just woke up one day and here I found myself, drunk and fallen off my horse, I guess. My horse had run off, but I had my saddle. I figured I'd either lost my horse or found a saddle. It was a mystery to me."

Old Pablo also believed in spirits, both holy and unholy. He thought it unwise to sleep during a full moon and that his liver turned over twice a year—spring and autumn.

"I think I once fornicated with a wolf in the form of a woman," he had told Cole, "and that she put a spell on my family because my own brother went completely blind the next day and my uncle fell off his horse in the river and drowned. Her eyes glowed in the dark, too. Scared the *mierda* out of me."

Cole believed the old man had lived a very strange and interesting life.

So now Old Pablo came up to the cabin on his cheap horse and saddle, for he had perceived activity at the place and was lonesome for company and a taste of Cole's whiskey. He had brought along a pair of prairie chickens in a wheat sack for the table, believing as he did it was always best to give a gift when calling on his neighbor and friend. The last time he'd come he'd brought the rusted two-blade Barlow he'd found.

The weather had turned unusually pleasant for that time of the year the day Old Pablo rode up. Tom and Preacher Man had carried the supper table out into the yard, such as it was, and Franzetta had fixed a meal of stew and baked biscuits for their supper. Charley Hood sat at one end with his crutches propped up, and John Henry Cole at the other as the others gathered around. They were just preparing to dig in when Old Pablo reined in.

He looked grim, sitting atop that nag of his, his head covered with that big straw sombrero that was now frayed, and an old cracked-handled revolver tucked down into the waistband of his trousers. Franzetta felt a shiver go through her at the sight of him. Charley reached under the table and let his finger rest on the trigger of his own pistol. Tom simply stared as Cole stood and went over and shook Old Pablo's hand and told him to slide down and come and eat with them.

"I brought you some sage hens," he said, and handed the wheat sack with the fowl in them.

"Muchas gracias," Cole said, and laid them aside.

Cole then introduced Old Pablo all around and told him to take a seat.

"There's only four chairs," Old Pablo said.

"Take mine," Cole said. "I'll sit on a bucket." And he went and got one, and turned it upside down.

Old Pablo could hardly keep his eyes off Franzetta. He could not have counted accurately the number of days since he'd last seen a comely woman, or any woman at all for that matter. Dormant urges bubbled up inside him, urges he'd forgotten he'd even had.

"You see something there you like?" Charley finally said, having noticed the way Old Pablo stared at his wife.

"Sí."

Cole gave Charley a look and said: "More biscuits?"

Franzetta put a hand on Charley's arm, a warning touch telling him that everything was all right and not to let his jealousy get the best of him. Charley had always been a very jealous man about Franzetta, had always considered himself to have married above his raising. He didn't like any man talking to her or looking at her the way he saw Old Pablo doing. He set aside his fork and spoon and pushed away from the table, and went off a little ways to try and cool down his temper since Old Pablo was Cole's guest, otherwise he might have shot the man. It did not help any that Charley was still hobbled by his wounds and reliant upon crutches to get around. Even as old as that Mexican was, all he'd have had to do was push Charley off balance, and he'd be down in a heap.

Cole wandered over to where Charley stood hobbled on his crutches and rolled himself a shuck, and said: "You must forgive that old boy. He doesn't mean anything other than Franzetta is as pretty as a new-born colt. That old man has lived alone so many years, I imagine he's half starved for any sort of feminine beauty."

"That don't justify anything in my eyes," Charley said, his voice edged with anger.

"No, it probably doesn't. But, listen, you can consider yourself a fortunate man to have a woman that other men find attractive. You could be sitting in some soddy in the middle of Kansas with a woman so homely you'd have to wait till dark to fornicate with her."

In spite of his jealous anger, Charley smiled at this. "I guess you're right."

"Besides, even if Franzetta were a single woman and you weren't in the picture, what do you suppose an old boy his age could even do with a woman but look at her?"

"Nothing, I reckon."

"You want a shuck?"

"Sure."

Cole smoked while Charley built himself a cigarette, then Cole let him light his shuck off the one he was smoking, and soon enough things seemed back to normal, for Charley had realized he'd been foolish for getting angry at such a reprobate as Old Pablo in the first place.

"I'm just a dang' fool for that woman," Charley said.

"Nothing wrong with that," Cole replied. "We're all danged fools for one thing or another."

"I'm starting to get restless hanging around and doing nothing."

"Well, soon as we heal up good enough, we'll talk about it," Cole said.

"I just don't like being told what I should do and where I should go, especially by a bunch of paper collars."

"I don't like it, either, but there are innocent folks in that town who would probably suffer if we had stayed and Sam Starr brought his bunch of madmen with him and burned it because of us. If we're going to fight them, it has to be where innocent folks won't get hurt."

"A time of our choosing," Charley said.

"Exactly."

Then Tom and Preacher Man came out of the cabin after helping Franzetta clear the dishes and carry them inside. Preacher Man took up residence on the splitting stump to read his Bible in the last of the light, and Tom came over to where Cole and Charley stood, smoking. Old Pablo still sat watching Franzetta as she came and went; her backside especially intrigued him. The lift and fall of her hips beneath the gingham skirt dragged up fragments of old memories of other women and their backsides he had once known. At the same time Old Pablo wondered about the boy who wasn't all boy nor all man yet, either. Old Pablo could see without being told that this was John Henry Cole's son—they had the same unreadable eyes and were similar in build, the boy just a thinner version of Cole.

Tom didn't say anything at first to Cole or to Charley. He just listened to their palaver. "What sort of trouble are you-all in?" he said finally.

"You don't want to know," Charley said.

"Maybe I do."

This reply startled Charley, for until that moment he had assumed the boy to be rather timid.

"We ran into an ambush several days back and got shot up pretty good," Cole explained, then went on to tell him the rest of it, how they had been asked to leave Red Pony. "That's why we're here," Cole concluded.

For a long moment Tom didn't speak—he was a lot like his father in that way, would hear the situation, weigh and evaluate it, then speak. "Seems to me you-all are just delaying what's bound to happen sooner or later."

"Won't argue there," Cole said.

"We're not running, son," Charley said. "We're just hanging out for a while."

"How many of them are there?" Tom asked.

"Don't rightly know for sure," Cole said.

"Sounds like you might need an extra man then," Tom responded.

"No, this isn't your fight," Cole said.

"I guess I can make whatever fight I want to mine," Tom replied. "I'm a freeborn man, like you, and him"—pointing with his chin toward Charley—"even that Preacher Man."

"Can you handle that piece you're packing?" Charley said doubtfully, "or is that just for show?"

Charley did not yet know of the incident in Lusk, of the man that Tom had shot in self-defense.

"I think he knows how to handle himself," Cole affirmed.

Then Tom sauntered over to where his painted horse stood and rubbed its face and threaded his fingers through its mane, speaking to it all the while, his closest friend and companion now that his ma had died. That horse was about all he had left, he reckoned, and the thought of it wrapped around his heart like a dark fist. He just needed to be left alone with no need of talk about this or that, or who he was or wasn't. He absently touched the rosary that hung around his neck and lay inside his shirt. It had been his mother's rosary and she'd given it to him that night she told him to go and find John Henry, his father.

"God will be your companion," she'd said weakly.

He hadn't wanted to leave her and would not have except for her insistence.

"You will need someone when I'm gone," she'd said.

"No, I won't," he'd argued. "I don't need anybody but you. I want to stay here with you until. . . ." He could not finish the thought.

Her fevered hands had closed upon his hand when she put the rosary there in his palm. "Please, for me," she'd said.

She'd made him promise. And so he had gone in search of John Henry Cole. And now he had shot a man because he had a quick and fiery temper and there was nothing to be done about it. Maybe he would die with these men. Maybe that was his destiny. But, he told himself as he walked in the evening air, dying might not be the worst thing. How peaceful she'd looked at the moment of her death.

The dusk of evening deepened until the air itself became colored—a brown-rosy glow that settled in around them. And from some unseen place a great horned owl came swooping through the night, its heavy wings thudding the air as it went in search of rodents that would come out of their dens. With its uncanny night vision it would swoop down like an avenging angel and take life to sustain its own. And were a man to be asked the meaning of life, he might be told that the owl had the answer, that the cycle of life and death is a never-ending circle, and one thing is wedded to the other. Some die and some live, and in between death and life are miracles.

CHAPTER TWENTY-ONE

"I ain't no math whiz," Sam Starr said, "but I can count, and four ready guns is all we got left. One-Eye yonder is no more use to us than a two-legged horse . . . are you, One-Eye?"

One-Eye lingered on a pallet on the floor of the rock house, his ear shot off, his toe shot off, and an open bullet wound in his leg from the bank robbery. "I reckon I ain't no good at all, Sam. But I'd appreciate you don't take me out and finish me and leave me for the crows to eat my only eye like you done those lawdogs."

Sam seemed to contemplate the idea, then said: "Don't fret it, One-Eye. You still might be of some use to me yet."

One-Eye looked relieved.

"What'd you have in mind of doing?" Shorty asked.

"I'm mighty tired of being cooped up in this stinking place. It's been three, four weeks now, and we got that money that needs spending, or why the hell else did we steal it?" He looked around for approval, or to assert his thinking. "But I'm also thinking we need to recruit a couple more men to replace One-Eye and Gunnerson."

"To what aim?" Black Bill said, sitting at the table drinking a cup of Arbuckle's and picking coffee grounds from his teeth.

"To the aim I am going to kill John Henry Cole and be done with it."

Atticus Creed stood by the open door, keeping an eye over the open plain below. He glanced at Sam Starr, having already read his intentions, then studied the faces of the others. "You think that's a good idea?" Atticus said in a rarified challenge to Sam. Personally he was sick to death of murdering—lawmen or anyone else. He'd just as soon that they all stick to robbing banks or trains. He figured to start putting money away so that when the time came, he could ride off and not look back—go get his sweetheart out of Fort Smith and start an honest life somewhere.

Sam looked at Atticus, surprised he'd even said anything. "You think it's pure coincidence that after we ambushed that bunch that within a week or two a couple of lawdogs come up in here to kill us in our sleep? No, it was John Henry Cole's doing. I know that sum-bitch as well as I know anybody 'cause he's my half-brother."

This piece of news caught everyone by surprise, even the women who lazed around in states of undress, slatternly, with exhausted looks on their faces.

Shorty said: "I never knew you even had family."

" 'Course I got god-damn' family, how you think I came to be?"

Shorty looked puzzled.

Even the mention of this brought to Sam's mind the crazy aunt and old lust. More than anything, Sam wanted to prove to John Henry Cole that *he*, not Cole, was the better man.

"You don't think we're enough to kill him?" Black Bill said.

"You might think you're good enough to kill John Henry Cole. You might even wish you were good enough to kill him . . . but you ain't."

Bill scowled at such comments. As far as he was concerned, he was the equal of any man, Sam Starr included.

"Who you thinking on getting?" Shorty said.

"The Cox brothers out of Ardmore."

"We worked with them before," Shorty said. "Real hard bastards."

"You're going to burn that town down, ain't you?" Black Bill said.

Again Sam Starr looked at him with eyes that were devoid of any compassion. "You're a real bright boy, Bill. Real bright."

"I say it's a fool's errand. I say we head out of this country and go some place else and forget your god-damned plan."

"That what you think?"

"It is."

"Well, Fanny, you ain't the head of this bunch far as I know."

Black Bill took umbrage at being called such a name. He stood away from the table so suddenly he knocked over his cup of Arbuckle's. It came to that when men were cooped up together. They turned into snarling dogs, ready to fight over everything and anything.

His hand swooped for the revolver on his right hip, but Sam Starr said: "Don't, or I'll kill you!" Just that quick Sam Starr had his own revolver cocked and aimed, the muzzle pointed directly as Bill's face and not an iota of wavering, either. "You can go along, or I can leave you here," Sam said. "You can't beat me, and you sure as hell ain't gonna beat John Henry Cole. But if you are of the mind to try me, give it your best go ahead. I can easy enough find your replacement."

Black Bill was a head taller and forty pounds heavier than Sam Starr who stood a mere five foot seven inches and weighed barely a hundred and thirty pounds. But he had a big black heart beating in his scrawny chest and no pity in him. Bill as well as everyone in the gang was aware of Sam's mercilessness. Another moment passed between them, then Bill eased his hand away from his gun and said: "Shit, look what you made me do, spill my coffee."

Shorty gave a begrudging laugh and One-Eye did, too. Atticus simply watched, perhaps hoping Sam Starr and Black Bill would kill each other.

"I guess you best pour you another," Sam said, then eased the hammer down on his pistol before slowly holstering it.

They boarded the noon cannonball at Beaver to take them to Ardmore—four hardened men in long coats, carrying rifles and wearing pistols, and walked down the narrow aisle between the rows of seats in a passenger car painted green on the outside with gold lettering.

Kids stared at them, and their mothers warned them not to. Black Bill made a face at one little freckle-faced boy and started him whining.

Atticus said: "Jesus, you have to do that?"

Shorty wound his pocket watch till it would not wind, then held it to his ear; it had been broken for the better part of a year already.

The engineer tugged his whistle chord, and the conductor gave a final call of—"All aboard!"—and the train started with a jerk, then seemed to settle, then gave a second tug until it was in motion. The station and the little town slipped away and the conductor came down the aisle, collecting tickets.

Sam and Bill and Shorty and Atticus had stuck their tickets in the bands of their hats once they'd settled in.

Soon the train reached its traveling speed and rocked gently from side to side on well-oiled springs thick as a man's leg. A child toward the back of the car began to cry and its mother tried to soothe it. Somebody coughed, and one of the passenger's rattled open the pages of a newspaper with print so small it was hard to read without spectacles.

The headlines read: *President Garfield Dies From Assassins Bullets. A Day of Mourning!*

Of course not a single member of the bunch could read, so to them it just looked like black lettering. They rode on and into the late night, the train rocking, the child whimpering, the killers at rest.

Chapter Twenty-Two

The marshal rode out from Lusk on a sweated bay horse. Old Pablo took refuge in the shed when he saw it was a lawman. A person with Old Pablo's history just naturally took to hiding when a lawman showed up. Past crimes he might have committed could still be on the books somewhere and faded dodgers had a way of reappearing.

Tom had seen him coming, too, and so had Cole. Preacher Man was off walking and reading his Bible as was his routine three or four times a day. He believed a man had to stay in the Word, lest he lose himself and forget his spiritual nature.

"Wait inside the cabin," Cole said to Tom.

"No, sir. If whatever it is he's come for has to do with me and what happened, I'll face him."

"Then we'll face him together," Cole said.

So they did.

The marshal was a middle-aged man with a belly that hung over his belt buckle as though he had a sack of grain under his shirt. His iron-gray sideburns came down to his jaw line and it was easy to see his nose had been broken several times by its mashed in and crooked shape. He dismounted without saying anything and stood for a second, holding the reins of his mount.

"Came to let you know that that fellow you shot the other night . . . T. Bone Blue . . . well, he's gonna live, but he ain't never gonna walk no more. Your bullet broke his spine."

"I'm mighty sorry for that, Marshal," Tom said. "I wished it didn't have to be that way, that he'd let it go."

"Well, it is what it is, and after doing some more investigating on it, I've no reason to hold you for anything further. Some just come to grief by their very nature. Just thought I'd let you know."

"Coffee, Marshal?" Cole asked.

"I'd appreciate it, but mind if I water my animal first."

Cole nodded toward the water tank, and the marshal walked his horse over and let it drink its fill, then dropped the reins, knowing it would stand without being tied. He came into the cabin where Franzetta had poured him a cup of Arbuckle's.

"There is another reason I rode out here," the marshal said as he blew steam from his coffee.

"Speak plain," Cole said.

"Well, let me just say that even the devil has his disciples, if you know what I mean. And T. Bone Blue certainly is a devil of a man, and he most certainly has run with his own kind over the years. I know he's mighty grieved for the condition you put him in, son"—the marshal looked over at Tom—"and I would not be at all surprised if he were to hire someone to come and kill you. So there you have it, full bore."

Tom seemed undisturbed by the warning. "Let whoever he sends come."

"It ain't like an assassin will walk up to you and introduce himself," the lawman said. "This country is full of assassins who will shoot you from hiding up to a quarter of a mile away. I've seen it."

"We'll keep an eye out for things," Cole said.

"It'd be best," the marshal said. Then: "This is mighty fine coffee, ma'am."

"Thank you," Franzetta said.

"This is a nice place you have here," he told Cole. "Name's Ben Morgan, by the way."

"It was decent of you to tell us the news about that fellow," Cole said. "My boy ain't a killer or trouble-maker."

Preacher Man came in just then, and stood by the stove.

"You mind if I ask what you-all are doing out here?" The marshal said this after taking in the others in the room, Charley and Franzetta, Cole, Tom, and now Preacher Man. It seemed to him somewhat odd, four fellows living with one woman. He hadn't seen anything like it but once before in a gold camp up in Colorado when he'd gone up there to strike it rich and never did. He'd known these two miners who stayed shacked up with a woman and they were the envy of the gold camp. He never did learn the details, but he'd have given half a week's wages to have learned them. He himself was a solitary man, and would never abide sharing a woman with another man. It just seemed somehow a sinful act that violated all of Nature's order.

"This is my place," Cole answered the marshal's question. "These are my friends, and this my son."

"Well, I best get back," the lawman said, standing abruptly. "Got plenty to do . . . plenty . . . shooting dogs and collecting taxes." He said this with a grin that made his face seem made of rubber.

Cole walked him out to his horse and watched him heft his bulk on board.

"You-all aren't Mormons, are you?" the marshal inquired.

Cole shook his head. "We're not anything, just people."

"Just wondering, is all," the lawman said, reined his mount around, and headed back the way he'd come.

Cole stood, smiling. *Mormons,* he thought.

Cole's shoulder still ached when he raised his arm too high, but his side was healing fine, just a little stitch when he moved awkwardly. Charley still had troubles getting around without his crutches and the only way he'd be any good in a fight, Cole reasoned, would be if he could be sitting down. The trouble was, it's hard to find a good gunfight where they'll let you sit down.

On the other hand, Cole was hoping that Sam Starr wouldn't follow through with his threats and was by now a long way from Red Pony, heading farther away still. Cole figured he could always track down Sam and his bunch. He knew Sam Starr as well as he knew anyone and a lot more than he liked. He wondered, if and when it came to it and he had the chance to pull the trigger on Sam, whether he could do it without hesitation. What if Sam pleaded for his life, invoked the name of their mother? It gave him pause for thought. He knew what the answer would be if it turned out the other way around. Sam would not hesitate. Now, too, there was this new business, this possibility that T. Bone Blue would hire a man to assassinate Tom. It seemed like once trouble started dogging you, it just never quit.

Cole went inside and got a pair of pistols and a box of shells, and walked off a distance from the house where he took aim at an old peach can that lay, rusted, a dozen yards away and set to shooting it because a man who makes his living by using a gun needs to keep his skills finely tuned. It was no different than a violinist who practices for hours each day. The pop and crack of his revolvers drew the others from the cabin, Preacher Man and Tom, and even Old Pablo, who'd left the refuge of the shed now that the marshal had ridden off. Charley came swinging on his crutches. Soon enough they were all firing their weapons at that old peach can, causing it to jump and dance like something alive.

Franzetta watched from the doorway of the cabin. She hated to admit to herself that there was something powerful about men firing guns together for a common cause. She admired Charley greatly, but truth be told, it was John Henry Cole who fascinated her the most. She had never before felt it as strongly as she did just then, not even during their brief encounter before Charley came along. But lately she'd begun to think about Cole more and more, had felt herself being irresistibly drawn to him, even to the point of hoping he would look at her in a certain way so that she could tell he was thinking about her in that way. And if so, perhaps at least he'd be willing to talk to her in private about it. But thus far Cole had seemed to ignore her, had avoided being around her alone. He was polite but distant, and it made her all the more want to be with him.

But on the other hand, she told herself, she was being foolish, that it was just the stress and fear of what might happen. She told herself that it had nothing to do with seeing Charley hobbling around on crutches like some old man. Since he'd been shot, they had not made love; he hadn't touched her. Getting shot seemed to have aged him ten years. There was already a fifteen-year difference in their ages. She could understand how a man hurting doesn't have such things on his mind like making love to his wife. She could understand it, but that didn't mean that she accepted it.

Damn you, John Henry, for being who you are, she told herself. *Why couldn't you have loved me the way that Charley does?*

Of the men firing their guns, Cole stood the tallest, his shoulders the broadest; his was the longest shadow cast over the ground. Cole was the looming figure among them all, and it was he who her gaze was fixed upon, he who caused her to have such crazy thoughts. She told herself, warned herself, that if she did not get herself and Charley gone from this place, and gone soon, that she could not vouch for what she might do, what might happen. She would speak with Charley that night, in bed once the others were asleep. She would tell him what they must do, and make him do it. Her hands trembled, and she turned away from the doorway and went to lie down on the bed, trying not to think of John Henry Cole. But think of him she did, and soon more than her hands trembled.

Chapter Twenty-Three

They stepped off the train in Ardmore, a dog-spit place full of lurking types, men with watchful eyes. *Opportunists,* Black Bill thought, looking about amid the steam and chuff of the train's big black engine.

They walked two by two down the street toward the center of town, Sam and Shorty in front, Atticus and Bill behind. Sam Starr had said he had a friend who owned a saloon—The Hair of the Dog—if he hadn't sold out or been killed, and if Mace Eddings was still around, he'd have a lead on finding some gun hands.

There wasn't anything to distinguish Ardmore for a dozen other towns in the Nations. It was just a place to get a whiskey, if you weren't an Indian, or a woman, or a card game. There was a hotel and several saloons and a couple of cathouses. There was also the usual hardware store, two to be exact, and medical offices—both dentist and doctor—a small infirmary, a three-cell jail made of brick, a bank, and so forth.

"This is the place," Sam said as he turned into the saloon, twisted the handle on one of the doors, and stepped inside. The others followed.

It was not yet noon and there was hardly anyone in the place. It had sawdust on the puncheon floors, a tin-stamped ceiling, a long oak bar to the right with shelves holding bottles of mixed cocktails, whiskey, and gin, three beer taps, and a double back-bar mirror. There were tables and chairs toward the back under mounted buffalo heads and one of an antelope. There was currently no indication of the rowdy nights when men crowded the bar to drink and laugh and gamble and fight. All was quiet. Mace Eddings stood behind the bar, reading the latest issue of *Harper's Weekly* about the assassination and subsequent death of President Garfield, how the poor man had suffered for weeks.

Eddings looked up at the entrance of Sam Starr and the others. What he saw he did not care for. He instantly thought of that sawed-off double-barrel he kept under the bar, the one he had used when he was a stage messenger. The only thing he'd ever shot with it was coyotes. He was by nature a peaceable man, although he hadn't always been so. There had been a time when he'd been a prize fighter and had the face to prove it. Nowadays, however, he considered himself a legitimate businessman who did not water down the drinks and gave fair measure. He brooked no fights inside the bar and had an oak billy club filled with lead in case a fist didn't do it and a shotgun was too much.

"Mace," Sam said as the lot of them bellied up to the bar.

"Sam," the mustached barkeep said coolly.

"See you're still wetting their whistles."

"Plainly."

"How about a round for me and my boys."

"What's your poison?"

"How about your best whiskey with a beer back for me and the boys?"

The barkeep poured and stood watching as they took their time tossing them back before going to work on the beers.

"What brings you boys to Ardmore?" Mace asked.

"Looking for the Cox brothers," Sam replied. "They around?"

"Could be."

"Like to offer them jobs."

"You plan on starting your own army?" Mace said, looking at the others.

"That's a thought," Sam said. "But, no, just have a job that requires more than the four of us. Reason I come here, to talk to you, was to see if you could put me onto those boys. I worked with them before."

"So I heard."

There was a visible tension between the two men. Mace would just as soon they hit the road and was not overly forthcoming until Sam Starr took $50 of that stolen bank money and counted it out right there atop the wood.

Sam said: "For your trouble, Mace. Might be more where that come from."

"I might know where they're at."

"You want to go round them up and bring them back here?"

"Lose money if everybody who walked through that door wanted me to run errands for them."

Sam put another $50 atop the wood. "Just set the bottle here while you go get them."

Mace scooped up the money and stuffed it in his waistcoat pocket. He hadn't wanted any truck with Sam Starr, but those greenbacks argued differently with him. Those greenbacks spoke a language all their own.

"Gimpy!" he shouted, and a fellow who'd been sitting at a table came up from the back, limping on a stiff leg. "Watch the bar while I'm gone," Mace ordered.

"Sure, boss."

"Sort of looks like One-Eye, don't he, the way's he's hamstrung," Shorty said, making light of the man's infirmity.

Mace left. Half an hour passed.

"The boys here are horned up," Sam said to Gimpy. "What's a good hog farm?"

"There's two here in town, and one out of town a couple of

miles. You want fat, or skinny, white or Chinese?"

"Hell if it matters," Sam said, looking at the others. Only Atticus Creed seemed disinterested. The outlaw life had worn thin on him.

"Then I'd recommend Miss Patsy's . . . she's got a good variety and keeps her girl's clean by having Doc Peters check 'em out about once a month."

"Doc Peters?" Shorty said. "Now that's a hell of a handle for a man who checks out beaver to see if it's clean or not!" Again, all but Atticus joined in on the humor.

"Point the way," Sam Starr said.

Gimpy told them how to get to Miss Patsy's—it wasn't far—but Atticus said he'd stay in the saloon and wait for the barkeep and the Cox brothers. The others left, and Atticus asked if Gimpy had any coffee. He said: "My head's swimming and I don't rightly like not being in my right mind."

Gimpy said he'd fix a pot. When he had done it, he brought Atticus a cup, and set it there on the wood.

"Sounds like you boys got something working," Gimpy said conspiratorially. "I'd be available for a job of any kind if you boys is hiring."

Atticus looked at the thin face with its bulging eyes. "I got no say in it," he said.

"Shit fire, fellow, I could use me some extra work. I ain't above breaking the law, neither."

Atticus said: "You ought to get on away from me now, mister."

"I know who that is you're with . . . it's Sam Starr, and that other one is Black Bill, too."

"How do you know such things?"

"Let's just say I do, is all I'm saying."

"Go on now, get away from me."

"Sure, sure, mister."

Gimpy went to the far end of the bar, and Atticus took his

coffee cup and went and sat at a table. A few minutes later Mace and the Cox brothers entered. Atticus had heard about them but never before had laid eyes on either one. They looked like cowpunchers the way they were dressed—sweat-stained sombreros, jackets over waistcoats over striped shirts, with big kerchiefs draped around their necks, filthy dungarees tucked down into the shafts of rough low-heeled boots. Atticus studied them. He could see by the bulges under their coats they were armed.

Their faces and hands were dark from sun and wind and the skin around their cheeks was as shiny as wax. One had a healed-over scar that ran from his ear to his jaw. They wore kidskin gloves and pulled them off, and tucked them inside their gun belts in order to drink. They looked about loosely at whoever else was inside the bar, cautiously, the way men who are either on the prod or on the dodge will do. Their gaze came to rest on Atticus and lingered there for a moment, then shifted back to the gimpy barkeep and their own images in the backbar mirror. They ordered whiskey with a beer back and stood talking among themselves.

Mace walked over to Atticus. "Where'd Starr go?"

Before Atticus could answer, Gimpy at the bar spoke up and said: "They went to buy pussy over to Miss Patsy's."

Mace's features showed displeasure. He said to Atticus: "I thought you boys wanted to do business with these fellows." He shifted his gaze to the Cox brothers who'd thumbed back their hats and stood drinking casually.

"I guess you'll have to take that up with Sam when he gets back," Atticus said.

Mace walked over to the bar and spoke to the Cox brothers. They picked up their drinks and sauntered over and stood before Atticus, He did not move or flinch or turn his gaze from theirs. Instead, his finger rested in the curve of the Winchester's trigger.

"Sam says you're looking to hire a couple of hands," the one with the scar said. They looked so much alike it would have been hard to distinguish one from the other were it not for the scar.

"Not me," Atticus said. "Them I'm with do."

"You ain't the hiring man, then?" the other said.

"I ain't nothing but me," Atticus said.

The two of them exchanged puzzled looks.

"How come you to say to Mace then that you was looking to hire hands?"

"I didn't say nothing to Mace."

The one with the scar looked over his shoulder toward Mace, who now stood behind the bar with both palms planted atop its surface, then brought his look back around to Atticus. "You're either hiring, or you ain't," he said.

Atticus considered the fellow more than stupid, the way some fellows are: of low education and no ambition to get any smarter, men who are content to live simply and without complications, men who are visceral in their behavior, whose words are based upon mood and not reason. Such men were not to be fooled with unless you were prepared to fight them at the drop of a hat. Such men were constantly ready to kill at the slightest provocation and sometimes with no provocation at all. The Cox brothers were the sort of men who lived hand to mouth, getting by on what they could beg, borrow, or steal. They more than likely drank and fornicated every red cent they ever had, and lived in between with empty pockets, brooding and scheming. Such men were little different than the beasts they rode, roped, or slaughtered, and maybe not even as smart. Such men did not build railroads or empires. They did not sing with mouths full of sun and flint. They were just a couple of common waddies, as far as Atticus could tell.

"Ask you again, you hiring, or ain't you?"

Atticus shook his head negatively only slightly, ready to blow them out of their boots, for he cared not a wit for either of them. "I ain't, but he is," Atticus said as Sam and the others came rattling through the doors just then.

They came over and gathered around, and Sam had two more bottles brought over by Mace. They all sat down at the table and palavered with Sam Starr doing most of the negotiating.

The Cox brothers seemed more than eager to pitch in with the gang for what Sam offered them. He finally introduced them to those who didn't know them—July and Wordell Cox. Sam Starr then asked as an afterthought: "What sort of name is Wordell?"

The brother without a scar narrowed his gaze and said: "It's one my mama gave me. You got a problem with it all of a sudden?"

"Just testing your feist," Sam said. "Have another glass."

"How far is this woebegone place, this Red Pony, anyway?" asked July Cox. "Never even heard of it."

"It's a fair to middling ride by train that will take us to Bever, and from there we'll go by horseback."

The Cox brothers had sandy hair with sharply receding hairlines. They had faces like those of churlish youngsters with gray-green eyes that didn't seem to set right, as though each eye was looking off to the side. Wordell had buck teeth, but July had his front ones missing altogether, another distinguishing feature along with the scar. They smelled of horse and sweat and had black dirt under their fingernails and in the creases around their eyes. July wore a silver pinky ring, and he cursed a lot, as if everything spoken or said surprised him and caused him to retort. They studied Black Bill as if he was some horse they were thinking about buying.

"What are you?" Wordell said.

"I don't catch your meaning," Bill said, even though he understood perfectly the question.

"I mean, you a nigger or Injun or Mex or what, exactly?"

"I'm a killer is all you need to know about me," Bill said, and calmly lifted his glass and swallowed it like a man might swallow a raw egg.

July hooted and slapped the table and said: "God damn!"

Shorty sat with his arms crossed over his chest, studying them, then said: "I met you boys once over in Tulsa."

"Yeah, when was that?" July said as if he was being accused of something.

"Five, six years ago. You was working 'punchers and got into a terrible big row in a bar there. Shot some fellows, then fled."

"We wasn't never in Tulsa, god damn!"

"I bet they still got warrants for you over that way."

"What you trying to prove, mister?" Wordell put in.

"Nothing. Just saying."

"Say nothing and you'll be all right."

"Say shit, and *you'll* be all right."

"That's enough," Sam Starr commanded. "We din't come here to start a fight."

An unsettling silence befell them, every man ready to pull the trigger if provoked further, but in the end money spoke much louder than any words, or any grievances they might carry, one for the other. They were uneasy badgers locked in a cage of their own making, one constructed of greed and ignorance and murderous inclinations.

"We'll leave on the noon flyer tomorrow. Be down at the train depot in time," Sam said.

"Could use us a little taste of that sugar now," Wordell suggested.

Sam Starr gave them $100. He was feeling most generous,

knowing there would always be more where that came from, and to meet his end of killing John Henry Cole and any who rode with him.

Near midnight, Shorty said: "I believe that trollop gave me the crabs."

Nobody laughed.

Atticus dreamed of far-off calmer places where the wind whispered through the corn and moths fluttered in the light of windows and crickets chirped in the dark. The whiskey was warm and peaceful in his blood now. He stroked his mustaches as he might a pet and saw himself surrounded by strangers and blood-letters and felt as if he was different from them somehow, even though he knew for certain that he was *indeed* one of them, and maybe the worst of them. He didn't know if he could ever make his way back to that place of his youth where the wind whispered through the corn and crickets chirped in the night.

Sometime during the dead of night they all drifted away and into sleep down at the local hotel and woke with heavy heads again in the morning and made their way to the depot where they lounged about like lazy cats while awaiting the sharp shriek of the flyer.

In passing, one of the local deputies spotted them—six heavily armed men—and, although there was a town ordinance against the carrying of firearms within the town's limits, the deputy judiciously decided to by-pass them and go on about his business.

And soon enough the train announced its coming via the engineer's whistle and chuffs of black smoke that dotted the sky.

"Come, let's go," Sam Starr said. "To our glory."

No one man among them knew what the hell exactly Sam was talking about. But it didn't matter.

CHAPTER TWENTY-FOUR

Before having left town, Sam Starr wired the sheriff of Red Pony a cryptic telegram that stated simply:

We are coming. STOP. Will arrive in 5 days time. STOP. Let Cole know to be there and ready for a fight. STOP. Else you and the rest shall suffer. STOP.

Town Marshal Lou Ford was a giant of a man who stood well over six feet four inches tall and had to duck under most doorways to enter a room. He neither drank nor smoked or chewed tobacco. He was faithful to his wife Katy and had been married to her for twenty years. On the very next day he went with her down to the river and let a preacher baptize him in the muddy brown waters of the Canadian.

It had been her suggestion. "We must walk in the way of the Lord," she'd said.

Lou knew it was true. That he had to take off his old clothes and be born again. They had moved two dozen times during their marriage because of Lou's search for a better job. He had prospected and worked in a lumberyard and traded horses. He had clerked in a store and apprenticed as a barber, something he didn't care a whit about. He had tended bar, and worked as a shotgun messenger for Wells, Fargo. He had worked for a time as a bordello inspector and a bank guard. No work had seemed to suit him and he was forever in search of a job that did. It wasn't until Lou answered an advertisement for a town marshal in Red Pony that he found his calling and eventually was offered the job.

"It seems like a nice quiet little town, Lou," Katy had said when she had first seen it.

"I believe it is," Lou had said.

He had been on the job for nearly three years by the time the bad business with John Henry Cole and his men came to pass. Lou Ford knew Cole and liked the man, as he did the others who worked for him. Lou also liked the fact that they were manhunters, and like any hunter kept the game farther and farther out and away from Red Pony, which made Lou's job that much easier and safer.

Lou Ford didn't care much about going after outlaws, wished in fact they didn't exist at all. His badge alone seemed enough to exert his authority in most local disputes. Besides, he was good with his fists in case he needed them. And sometimes he *did* need them to break up a drunken fight. He could hit like a mule, and after a while word got around and troublemakers soon gave him his due when he waded in among them. It was a nice clean life and Lou Ford planned to live long enough to be able to retire.

Katy was a member of the Presbyterian Church and sang in the choir and volunteered at the infirmary and got on teaching at the school. She and other of the churchwomen held pie dances and picnics and such and did what they could to help make Red Pony a decent place to live. She urged Lou to rid the place of the "bad element", not that there was that much there— just one bawdy house with three working girls to satisfy the needs of ranch hands and cowpunchers when they came to town.

Lou explained to her that it was easier to control men if they were allowed their vices, and that, as long as no real trouble started, it was better to allow a little gambling and whoring and some drinking than to try and cut it off altogether.

Katy did not fully buy Lou's reasoning, but Lou was her husband and her beliefs called for her to obey her husband, and so she did but without enthusiasm when it came to certain things.

The telegram, when it arrived, was not unexpected, but it was depressing. Lou's good life seemed threatened, his and Katy's and the rest of the townfolks', most of whom Lou considered friends. He read the telegram three times over as he paced in his small office there on Main Street. Soon enough word would spread all over town, from mouth to mouth because Donally, the telegrapher, would spread it. The town council and others would be pounding on his door demanding to know what he was going to do about it. What could he do about it?

Lou left his office and went home and talked to Katy and expressed his fears that the Sam Starr gang would show up and start shooting innocent people and there was nothing he could do to stop it—that the streets would run red with the blood of men, women, and children.

She said: "Let us pray about it, Lou."

"What good will praying about it do?" he said sourly. "God won't stop them. You might think that He will, but He won't."

"Lou," she said, "have you lost your faith in our Lord Jesus?"

"I never had it," he confessed. "I thought I had it, there for a while, but I didn't."

Lou Ford held a very deep dark secret from long years past, long before he ever met Katy. The secret resided in him like a black tumor. He tried hard not to think of it and sometimes could go for weeks and weeks without the cloud of it darkening his thoughts. But then something, usually from some little innocuous incident, would make him think about it and his mood

175

would plummet and he'd have to struggle hard to get it back up again.

Now with the telegram in his hand he felt the darkening of his mood again, felt as if because of his sinful secret he was having to pay, perhaps with his life this time, for what he'd done so many years ago. He thought: *I was just a wiseacre kid, what'd I know about anything? And haven't I been decent ever since? Ain't I tried?* He knew that he could just quit and leave, of course, start over. He and Katy were getting on in years, no longer young, but maybe they could start over. "Maybe we ought to pack up and get out of here," he hinted.

She looked at him with her startled china-blue eyes and said: "Lou, what are you talking about? We can't leave our home . . . these good folks who've come to be our friends, my duties at the church and the school. . . ."

He knew the moment he'd suggested leaving he shouldn't have. No, this burden was on his shoulders and his back and he'd have to carry it and see it through till the end, no matter. "You're right," he told Katy. "I don't know what I was thinking about."

Her face relaxed. "It will be fine, Lou. Things will work out, you'll see. Jesus will send us an answer to all this mess and things will be fine."

He went out again and found his two deputies eating lunch in the café and sat down between them, and said in a low voice: "Boys, we got trouble brewing." And they wondered: "What sort of trouble, Lou?" And he showed them the telegram, saying to keep it to themselves. First Jim Dander read it, and then Hal Biggs read it. Troubled looks gathered in their faces, much like a storm that comes up suddenly when one minute the sky is bright and clear and beautiful and the next it is full of dark rain clouds and the wind has kicked up hard.

"Well, we sort of figured it might come to this, didn't we,

Lou?" Jim Dander said in his raspy voice.

"We sort of did, I reckon," Lou said. "But now it's no longer simply an idle threat. They're actually coming."

Hal Biggs scratched behind his ear, tipping his hat forward, then readjusted it so it didn't set so low over his eyes. He was a rotund man who'd once jumped off a railroad bridge into the Niobrara River in Nebraska on a bet with a pig farmer that he wouldn't do it and broke his ankle. It never did set right and he had a limp forever on account of it. "Boy, I don't see how I can do this for fifty dollars a month," he said, wiping his mouth with his napkin. Suddenly his stew didn't taste so good. The thought of getting a bullet, maybe in the belly, just raised the bile in him. "Reckon I'll have to resign, Lou," he said. "I'm just not up to such violence as what it seems is promised in that telegram."

"You can't quit," Lou said.

"I don't see how you can stop me," Deputy Biggs said.

"If he quits," Jim Dander said, "that just leaves me and you, Lou."

"I'll deputize some men to stand with us."

But Jim, too, had already made up his mind and took off his badge and set it beside his coffee cup. "No, Lou, I got them three kids I'm having to raise since Mary Lee's been gone. What would them kids do without a daddy now that they've lost their mother?"

"I'll ride out and explain it to John Henry," Lou said. "He's a man of honor. He'll understand."

Hal Biggs unpinned his badge, too, and set it next to Jim's. "Maybe he will, but maybe he won't, Lou. He was smart, he'd ride clean to Canada and cross the border and stay there. That's what I'd do was I him."

"I can't believe you're both quitting me in my hour of need."

"I reckon each of us got to do whatever's best," Jim said.

"You ought to, too, Lou. You and Katy clear out while you can. Let someone else handle this mess."

Lou could see that girl plain as day now. How he and those other two boys had gotten her up in the barn that day when her daddy was gone off to town. Her name was Sylvia and she was not the prettiest thing around, but she'd been sweet on Lou and lived just over on the next place and up the road from him. They'd started sneaking off and going down to the creek and hiding in the tall grass, and how she'd said that first time: "I'll give it to you, Lou. I'll take off my dress, and give it to you if you want me to."

He'd never before lain with a gal but was of that age when a boy knows to rut and gets all fevered up, and if he's lucky, there's a gal he can get to rut with, such as Sylvia was with him that day and other days subsequently. It was a thing to brag about to his two best friends, Zeke Haskill and Roy Shepherd. He told them about it in great detail and they got after him to let them fool with her, too.

"Don't know that she will," he had said. "I think she'd just do it with me is all."

Just the thought of it knotted in his throat sitting there with his now ex-deputies. How she looked so frightened when they all three got her in that barn, up in the haymow, had her surrounded and insisted that she do it with all three of them. And when she started crying and refused and asked to be let go, Lou had begged and then cajoled her, telling her there was no difference whether it was just him, or him and his friends, too, that fornicating was fornicating and didn't she see the reason in it? And she said no, she did not see it that way, and please to let her go. He kept telling her that it would just be that one time, that's all. Just that one time.

"No, Lou," she had said. She had said it pleadingly at first, and then angrily when he wouldn't leave off. She was crying and begging them to leave her go, but by then it was way too late, for they'd unloosed the straps to their coveralls and were all fevered up, their brains on fire with lust. They circled her like wolves, closing her in an ever tighter circle, still trying to convince her to go along with their wants. They took her hands and rubbed them on themselves.

When she'd tried to scream, Zeke had fallen upon her, his hand clasped over her mouth, and then Roy had got her by the legs, those kicking legs, and held her. Lou had felt unable to move at first, then he had begun to tremble. He had watched the other two take what they wanted, and when Roy finished with her, he had said: "Your turn, Lou."

"No," he'd said. "Let her go."

"We will, soon as you take your turn."

"I don't want no turn."

"Hell, I guess you don't, since you've already been getting it. But this time you take your turn so in case she blames me and Zeke, she'll have to blame you, too."

"No," he had said again.

"You either do it or we're gonna beat the hell out of you and pitch you off this hayloft and listen to your damn' bones break. Then we'll pitch her off, too."

So he had done it. It had been bad enough he had done it and they had watched. But he had half enjoyed doing it. That was the worst part. And when he'd finished, they'd laughed and warned the girl not to say anything or else they'd come back and take it out on her again, only this time worse, and they'd keep doing it until she kept her mouth shut.

Then those two had left and Lou and she had been alone, and he had to listen to her sobs, had to look into her red, swollen eyes. They'd torn her dress and blood was smeared on her legs. He'd said in deep shame: "I'll make it up to you, Sylvia. I swear I will." But he'd never got that chance because a week later she'd hanged herself in that same barn.

He had gone and found Roy and Zeke, had waylaid them in fact, and busted them good with a length of oak limb, cursing them as he'd beaten them, busted teeth, and broke noses. He'd made them pay, but there was no kind of pay that would make up for what they'd done.

It had been the blackest moment of his life and not one he could ever get over and that was a pitiful feeling, to do something you could never forget and never get over, something that you carried around inside you and was a scar on your soul. So he'd run away, hopped a freight train and several more until he was so far from home he figured nobody would ever find him again. He hated running. And now it looked as if he had to run away again, or stand and fight and probably die for something or someone he had little truck with. It sure enough seemed like his sin had caught up to him.

He sat there, staring at the badges. Jim Dander and Hal Biggs had gone during Lou's reverie about what had happened. He felt now as alone and fearful as Sylvia must have felt up in that barn with boys setting upon her. The vision of her blood-streaked thighs sickened him even now. *Buck up,* he told himself. *Buck up. Do what you got to do but do it quick.*

He stood, began to walk out, and saw himself in the plate-glass window as he passed by, a watery reflection of a troubled man. He went to the livery and got his horse and saddled it and rode forth, perhaps on a fool's mission. He told himself the whole way: *Buck up. Don't quail.*

The wind was cold and sharp, cutting across the flatland so that Lou had to put his collar up and tuck his chin down into his coat. It made him feel small and even frail, like a kid, like that boy again, her blood dried and sticking to his hands. And later the blood of his two friends as he beat them with the tree limb seemed not to have ever washed from his mind. *What are you capable of, Lou? Murder? Maybe. Well, there is only one person who can help you. John Henry Cole. You have to convince him to come back and offer himself up to Sam Starr and his gang. You have to convince him that he must sacrifice himself to save the town. You can do it. You can talk him into it. Explain how a man should do the right thing even if it costs him personally. You know, don't you, Lou, what it's like to do a shameful act and be forever sorry for it. Well, that's what John Henry Cole would be doing if he tucked tail and ran off and didn't face down the Starr gang. You tell him without going into the details, Lou, how, if he doesn't do the right thing, he'll have to live with that shame all his life.*

He put the horse into a trot, and then into an easy lope. It was cold and he had a two-day ride ahead of him.

CHAPTER TWENTY-FIVE

That night Franzetta got Charley alone while the others were outside, Cole and Tom talking, Old Pablo getting drunk on the whiskey Cole had given him, and Preacher Man off by himself, meditating.

"Listen, Charley," she said, "I want us to get out of here as soon as possible."

"Where do you want us to go, Franny?"

"I don't care . . . anywhere but here."

"You afraid Sam Starr will come and find us here?"

"I'm not afraid of anything. I just don't want to stay here any longer."

Charley sat on the side of the bed, his crutches crossed upon his lap. "I love you, Franny. Love you to death. But I got to stand by John Henry."

"Oh, don't be a damned fool!"

This surprised Charley, her sudden anger. He didn't understand where it was coming from. "I'm no fool," he said. "Leastways not about this."

Franzetta's fists were balled so tightly her knuckles showed white. "You don't understand."

"Understand what? What is it eating at you?"

"Oh, nothing, damn it. Just nothing at all."

Charley said—"I need some night air."—and hobbled out, leaning on his crutches and cursing his wounds for making him seem old and feel so feeble.

Light from inside the house spilled out onto the ground, and it was enough light for the men outside to see about them. Preacher Man was now nearest the window in order to read his Bible.

Charley paused outside and stood, looking off at the star-salted sky and the scar of a moon, the night wind creating a chill. Smoke from Cole's cigarette blew upward and spread like wraiths looking for their ethereal home.

"I don't know what the hell is wrong with that woman," Charley remarked. "She's twisting me like a fresh-washed shirt."

"She doesn't want to see you killed, Charley," Cole said. "She's afraid of losing you."

"Is that it?"

Tom squatted on his heels nearby, playing mumblety-peg with a bone-handled clasp knife. He had become lost in his own thoughts, and Cole just let him be, figuring the boy was still wrestling with his emotions, either over the death of his mother, or shooting that fellow up in Lusk. In fact, Cole was a bit concerned about what might happen based upon what that sheriff had said. But then you never knew when it came to hardcase types whether they were bragging or meant it. *Well, hell,* he told himself, *I'm good and tired of folks threatening me and mine.*

"What do you want to do, Charley?" Cole asked. "You want to leave? If so, Preacher Man can drive you and Franzetta somewhere. I think she's right in wanting you to go, if that's what's got you upset. You can't blame her for that. You're not letting me down if you're worried about it."

"I know it," Charley said. "Where the hell'd that old Mex go?"

"Out there somewhere," Cole replied. "Was just here, but he comes and goes like the night wind. Why you asking?"

"I was hoping to get a taste of that lineament. You got another bottle stored somewhere?"

Cole shook his head negatively. "No, don't keep it except for Old Pablo."

"My nerves are raw," Charley said. "That's the only reason I could use a drink."

Preacher Man looked up from his reading and marked his place with a piece of red ribbon. "You want to leave with your wife," he said to Charley, "I'm glad to take you."

"She wants to go real bad."

"We can leave in the morning if you want."

"Let you know then, if it's all right. I'll talk to her some more."

Tom stood, folding his blade and putting the knife in a front pocket of his dungarees. Cole could tell the boy was now rest-less as all get out, like a wild young horse caught by a rope, knowing somebody was going to try and break it, and knowing it wouldn't let itself be broke. "Hell," he said, "why don't we just go and find those sons-a-bitches and take care of 'em?"

Cole realized then, perhaps really for the first time, that Tom was every bit his equal and the equal to any man among them. It was a harsh reality.

"Well?" Tom said, facing his father.

"Well, nothing," Cole said. "I'll decide when and where, but you stay out of it."

He saw the look on his boy's face then, a mixture of disap-pointment and anger. It seemed like everybody was getting slightly on edge.

Then a rider appeared out of the night, and Charley said: "Jesus, look what the cat's dragged in."

Lou Ford halted his mount and said: "John Henry. Charley."

"You come for supper?" Charley said. "Well, you're too late."

"Get on down, Lou," Cole said.

Tom stood staring, and so too did Preacher Man, who was

suddenly filled with the Holy Spirit, or at least it felt that way.

Lou Ford dismounted and said: "I hate to be the bearer of bad news, John Henry."

"Speak plain," Cole said.

Lou handed him the telegram and Cole tilted it toward the light and read it, then handed it back to Lou.

"You want me and Charley to come back and face them, is that it?"

Lou stood, holding the reins of his horse, lightly tapping them into one gloved hand, almost bashful it seemed to Cole, like a man asking a girl to dance with him.

"First you ask us to leave, then you ask us to come back," Charley chimed in. It had been an irritating evening for him thus far. The appearance of Lou Ford didn't help any.

"I'm just asking you to do the right thing, Charley, you and John Henry here."

"The right thing being to get gunned down in order to save that town that wouldn't stand behind us when we needed them."

Lou shifted his weight uneasily at the accusation because he knew it to be true. "I'm just one fellow," he said. "Hell, I don't even have any deputies. Roy and Zeke quit soon as they saw this. I imagine they've taken their families and are in the next county by now."

"Well, that about puts you in the jackpot now, don't it, Lou?" Charley wasn't about to let up.

Lou said: "You can abuse me all you want, it's not going to change a thing."

"You hungry, Lou?" Cole asked.

"I reckon I could stand to eat a biscuit if it had bacon lard smeared on it, and a cup of coffee before I head back."

"Tom, would you go and ask Franzetta to fix Lou here something to eat and get him a cup of coffee?"

Tom was anxious to do something.

Inside the cabin Franzetta was packing a bag for her and Charley, filling it with the few things they'd brought.

Tom said: "John Henry wanted me to ask you if you'd fix up something for this fellow outside to eat and make him a cup of coffee."

She looked at Tom, saw a young version of John Henry Cole, and his handsomeness swept through her like a wild wind. "What fellow?" she said.

"Some fellow named Lou is all I know."

"Lou Ford from Red Pony?"

"I reckon that's who it is."

"What'd he say he came here for?"

"Said he wanted John Henry and Charley to come back to Red Pony, reckon that's what."

The color drained from her already pale face. "Come back?"

Tom shifted his weight. She reminded him a little of his mother—a good-looking woman with a carriage that suited her and one that would draw a man's attention, not that he knew much about women, since he surely did not. "That's all I know," he said, and went out again, wanting to learn more about the situation.

Franzetta sat on the bed, holding her face in her hands and trying not to weep. *Sin, sin, sin,* she thought. *We are all, every last one of us, paying for our sins . . . Charley for his, John Henry for his, and me for mine.* She bit her lower lip, her faith being shaken. *How is it we pray and say we believe and tell ourselves that God watches over us and will protect us, and yet at the first sign of serious trouble, we doubt, as I am doubting now?* It seemed to Franzetta that faith was the most fragile of things, thin as an egg shell, as illusive as love itself. It seemed like God was only present when things were good.

She tried to tell herself that Charley and John Henry would not be killed if they faced down the Sam Starr gang. But she knew that they would be, and that she would not only find herself a widow, but that her truest love, John Henry, would exit this world without ever knowing how much she cared for him. It seemed such a shame, such a crying shame. For a long moment she gave into her fears, and then, as she'd always done in the past when things got their roughest, she steeled herself, wiped her eyes, stood, and went forth and fixed a biscuit with some salted ham on it and a cup of coffee and walked outside to give it to Lou Ford.

The air was black and cold as iron, and she wondered how they stood it, being outside, and why they would choose it simply to smoke and talk among themselves. Lou Ford looked at her with a hangdog expression that became even more hangdog when she handed him the sandwich and coffee and said quite coldly: "Lou."

He took it without speaking, for he knew what she had to be thinking.

"Charley's not going back with you, Lou," she said as Lou chewed his sandwich, the crumbs of the biscuit falling over the front of his shirt. Still he said nothing but merely looked at Charley who was himself looking a little forlorn.

Then she looked at Cole and said: "You're responsible for this. You tell Charley he can't go with you. You order him to stay here with me."

Charley spoke up and said: "That's enough, woman!"

She stood, hugging herself against the cold, against the fright, then turned and ran back into the cabin.

"Let me go talk to her, Charley," Cole said.

"I wish you would."

Cole found her sitting on the bed, trembling.

"Franzetta," he said.

She instantly jumped up and threw her arms about his neck and pressed herself to him. "It's you, John Henry. It's you I'm most worried about."

Her tears dampened the side of his face, her grip as strong as if he were saving her from drowning. He pulled her away and looked at her. "I don't understand what this is about."

"I've kept it long hidden, my feelings for you."

He held up a hand. "Much as I can appreciate that, it can't be. You are Charley's wife."

"We could go away, just ride clean out of the territory and not look back," she said with short, hard breaths. "We could go to Arizona, or maybe California, just the two of us, John Henry. It's what I want, what I've always wanted now that I've had time to think about it, now that I've seen you again."

"No," he said, shaking his head. "No, I couldn't ever do that to Charley, and I can't allow you to, either."

Suddenly she stiffened. "Me? You don't have a say over me or what I want or don't want. If I want to leave Charley, I will."

"Not with me," he said, and turned on his heel and walked back outside again.

"Well, you get her calmed down?" Charley asked when Cole rejoined them.

"I think so," Cole lied. "But hell, I'm not rightly sure."

"Women," Charley said.

Tom stood idly by with his hands slipped down into the back pockets of his jeans, ready to go to a fight. He didn't know why he even cared about his father and his troubles, or Charley, either. But his father had walked him away from trouble in Lusk, and truth be told Tom would like to find out John Henry's full story before he rode away, this man who he looked so much like, this man whose blood ran through his veins whether either of them liked it or not.

"Yeah, women," Cole said.

"What you-all gonna do?" Lou Ford said, having finished his sandwich and coffee, and tossed out the dregs.

"We'll let you know," Cole said.

Lou slapped the reins of his horse in his gloved hand again. "Well, I can't force you to come."

"That's right, Lou," Charley said. "You can't force us to do nothing."

Lou nodded, and forked his stud horse, tugged down his hat so low it bent the tops of his ears over, then turned the horse about and headed back the way he'd come, trusting the animal to make its way in the dark.

"There goes a rather lonesome and troubled man," Preacher Man said, having overheard the conversation.

Charley said: "You got anything in that holy book to tell us what we ought to do?"

"Take out thy sword and smite thine enemies left and right. And Samson roared . . . 'With a jaw of an ass I have slain a thousand men.' Seems to me you all should be able to finish off one lowly gang of criminals and miscreants."

Charley looked at Preacher Man as if he was daft. "Now where the hell are we going to find the jaw of an ass?" Then he turning his gaze quickly to Preacher Man's pair of Missouri mules.

Chapter Twenty-Six

T. Bone Blue moaned from his bed: "That bastard kid ruined me. He ruined me forever. I can't walk. I can't even feel my legs. Christ, bring me some whiskey, woman!"

Vineta had begun to contemplate life with T. Bone, with him now a cripple, and she still a young and viable woman. What would she have to do if she stayed with him, wait on him hand and foot? Be his nursemaid? Tote him around in a wheelbarrow?

"Oh, my God! Oh, my God!" he cried night and day. Doc had said to keep a diaper on him like a baby. She thought it should be her crying—*Oh, my God!*—night and day.

"I want him dead," T. Bone declared. "Go and find Duck Leslie and get him to come here."

So she went in search of Leslie, a man she had seen around and whose reputation was that of a low-brow rumored to have killed men for hire. He was first and foremost an ugly man, this Duck Leslie. Tall and thin with a beak of a nose, loose-lipped mouth, and weak chin—always a sign, Vineta thought, of perversion, weak chins. Duck was known to keep court up the street at the Three Aces Cattleman's Emporium. A mighty fancy name for such a dive. A sign out front nailed to the door declared: *No Unescorted Females.* She ignored it and went in anyway.

The place was patronized by weaklings and miscreants, layabouts and out-of-work cowboys. There wasn't a man worth a spit among them, she judged. And there at the far end of the bar stood Duck Leslie. He was hard to miss because of his

190

height and the sombrero he wore made him seem even taller than he was.

Curious eyes watched her with a high degree of anticipation, practically slavering all over themselves as she walked past. She ignored them completely, the barkeep, too, when he protested about her being in the place unescorted.

"Go to hell," she said. "I've come to see Duck."

Duck straightened to his full height from leaning on his elbows and eyed her suspiciously. He was suspicious of women in general, and most especially those who came into saloons looking for him. The last one who had, claimed she had a baby growing in her that was his. He had ridden a fast horse out of that town and landed here in Lusk.

"T. Bone wants you to come and see him," she said.

He looked down at her with his hooded eyes as though he was too lazy or stupid to open them all the way. She'd never seen such an ugly man. He was dressed in buckskin shirt and corduroy trousers that were soiled, a black and white cowhide vest with most of the hair worn off. He sported a pair of ivory-handled pistols stuck in a wide leather belt about his waist that reminded Vineta of a saddle cinch, and had a large red scarf draped around his neck that probably hadn't been washed in four years.

"Good god, but ain't you a pimp," she said.

"I take offense at you, madam," he said.

He even talked like a sissy, she thought, that high-pitched voice of his belying his size. "You can take it however you please," she said. "I don't give a rat's arse."

"Then I decline your invitation," he said imperiously.

"You can decline anything you want, but I reckon you'd be an ignoramus if you did so without first hearing his offer."

Now Duck Leslie lived mostly on the generosity of lesser men who wanted to hear all about his adventures with such as

Wild Bill Hickok and Texas Jack Omohundro. Duck Leslie could spin a yarn as good as some women could spin wool. The cost of admission was one drink per set of ears doing the listening.

Duck Leslie also told tales about such inamoratas as Big Nose Kate and Calamity Jane—said he and Wild Bill had once shook dice for the privilege of spending the night with Jane. He claimed a lot of lovers, among which was Squirrel Tooth Alice and Hair Lip Annie.

"Now, boys, there was one ugly toad of a woman."

Guffaws.

"But, boys, I tell you the truth, however, when it comes to ugly women. Turn out the lights and they all look the same."

More guffaws.

The man could sure stretch the truth and stretch a lie even more.

"Offer? What sort of offer?"

"Jesus and Mary, I'm not going to stand around in this outhouse and palaver with you. You want to come, come, else stay here and bedazzle these oafs and laggards."

Vineta turned and stalked out.

"Reckon I better go see what that damn' T. Bone wants of me," Duck Leslie said to the others who'd gathered around him like hogs to the slop trough. "Hold on there, little sister!" he called as he caught up to Vineta outside. She did not bother to slow down or wait but continued forth at a rapid pace back to the little house she rented with T. Bone—a house that had now become a prison of misery as far as she was concerned.

Duck liked the looks of the woman from behind and so slowed his pace in order to watch her all the way to the house. Inside, T. Bone was propped up in his bed with a stack of stained pillows. His eyes rolled toward the pair of them and suddenly he was jealous, thinking maybe Vineta and Duck Leslie had conspired to fornicate and carry on behind his back, or, worse, right in front of him. And what could he do about it if they had? *Not a single thing,* he told himself.

"Well, it's about time you two showed up," he growled through a grizzled face. "What you been up to behind my back?"

"Jesus." Vineta sighed and went back out again, leaving Duck Leslie and T. Bone to their own devices.

"What can I do you for?" Duck Leslie said.

"You look like something that belongs on a dime novel cover," T. Bone said.

"This shirt was give to me by Buffalo Bill Cody several years back," Duck Leslie said with false pride, for he'd bought the shirt in a Kansas City emporium.

"Well, it looks like you ain't washed it since," T. Bone said sourly.

"I din't come here to be insulted by some cripple."

" 'Course you din't."

"Then why did I come here?"

" 'Cause I got a proposition for you."

"Yeah, and what would that be?"

"Close that door. I don't want her hearing."

Duck Leslie closed the door.

"Now sit down here close to me, so I can talk low."

Duck scraped a chair over to the bedside and sat and wrinkled his nose at the sick smell of T. Bone—sort of a combination between an outhouse and an apothecary.

"I'll pay you two hundred dollars to track down that kid what shot me and put one in his skull."

Duck straightened as if he had a twitch in his backbone. "Whare'd someone like you get two hunnert dollars?"

"You don't worry about it," T. Bone said. "You want the damn' money or not?"

"And all I got to do is track this kid down and shoot him?"

"That's it . . . hunnert now and the other hunnert when the

job's done."

"How am I supposed to find one kid in all this country?"

"Easy. I had Vineta go question R.T. on it. He gave up the goods on that fellow, told her their names and where they're from . . . not more'n ten miles from here."

"I always knowed R.T. Dickens as a closed-mouth son-of-a-bitch," Duck said. "How'd she get him to give up the goods?"

"Don't you worry your damn' head none about it."

Duck figured he knew how Vineta had gotten the marshal to give up such information. Only one way a woman like her got a man to do anything—barter for beaver. "How you know I won't just take the money and abscond with it?"

"Abscond," T. Bone said. "That's a mighty big word, Duck. You even know what it means?"

"I know what it means."

" 'Cause if you was to *abscond* with it, I'd just hire a killer to track you down and kill you, is what."

Duck Leslie scratched his itching neck, and then his crotch, then up under one arm. "Deal," he said. "Killing don't mean nothing to me. All I've ever done in my life is kill people. It was I who tracked down Jack McCall after he shot my pal, Wild Bill, and put a bullet in him. Killing for money is the easiest thing I ever done."

"Except for lying."

Duck wrinkled his beak of a nose.

T. Bone reached under the sheets for the money he'd stolen from Vineta's hidden cache—her whoring money that she'd been saving for over a year. She'd planned on putting together a nice fat stake and then clearing out of the country and starting a new life. She knew how to play the piano and maybe she could teach such skills to children for a fee, become a prim and proper lady, and maybe marry a man who wore celluloid collars and neckties and scraped mud off his shoes before he came into the house. She'd had to screw a lot of drovers and teamsters and assorted other types for that money and as soon as she found it missing, she'd go crazy, T. Bone knew. She was a damned wildcat of a woman when her dander got up and might even stab him in the heart, were she to learn it was he who took her stake. Well, *he* wasn't going to tell her, and he made sure to swear Duck Leslie to secrecy as well.

"She asks what I wanted to see you for, make something up. You're good at lying."

"There you go with the damn' insults again."

"Swear," T. Bone said.

"Sure, no skin off my teeth."

"You come back with a newspaper clipping you killed that kid, you'll get the rest of the money."

"Let me ask you something," Duck said.

"What's that?"

"Supposing you were to die while I'm gone, how am I gonna get the rest of my money?"

"I ain't gonna die, you damn' twit. I look like I'm gonna die to you?"

"You look mighty peaked. I seen men die who don't look near as peaked as you."

"Oh, Christ, I guess it's just a gamble you're gonna have to take. You want that damn' hunnert dollars or not? If not, give it back, and I'll find me someone else for the job, and you can go back to begging for drinks and telling your damn' lies."

Duck suddenly pulled one of his pistols and cocked it and put the muzzle to T. Bone's skull.

"Maybe I ought to blow you out of that bed and go and fuck that woman of yours and take all your money, how'd that be?"

Then Duck heard the click of the hammer T. Bone thumbed back on a little double-shot Derringer that he also kept under the sheets, and said: "Well, I reckon you'd rather not die more'n me. I'm half ways to Hades already. You're choice, a bullet in your balls or the money."

Duck lowered the hammer on his piece and grinned, a row of blunt yellow teeth trapped within those rubbery lips of his, and said: "Sheeit, T. Bone, I was only jaking you."

"Well, don't jake me no more if you know what's good for you."

Duck stood clumsily and tugged down his sombrero and strode out the room, his spurs rattling like loose change in a church plate.

Vineta was there by the front window, looking out, smoking a cheroot, the smoke wreathing around her head, the light filtering through her thin dress so that he could see the shape of her and it caused him to lick his lips like a dog expecting to be tossed a pork bone with some meat still on it.

"You're a fine-looking woman," he said, coming up to her. "How much for a toss?"

She looked at him, ugly as he was, and shuddered. Still business was business, and she could use every red cent she could earn to add to her hidden money.

"For you, ten dollars," she said. "And no lingering one, either. Five minutes to get your gun off or else."

"Ten dollars? Hell, that's twic't the going rate. I can get it up the street from any whore in town for five."

"Then go up the street and get it and three days from now, when you can't squeeze out a drop of water without it feeling like razor blades coming out the end of your pizzle, you'll be wishing you'd never heard of them clap traps."

Duck knew she wasn't lying; he'd heard of how syphilitic most of Lusk's whores were. Almost everybody in Lusk knew to stay clear of them, but the outside cowboys and drummers traveling through were ignorant of the fact, and so the chippies continued to do a tolerable business, citing the only Latin any of them knew: *Caveat emptor.*

"Well," Duck said, "where you want to do it?"

The only bed was the one in which T. Bone lay stricken.

"How about just up against the wall," she said. "But I want my money before you put it in."

"Suits me," Duck said, and unwittingly gave Vineta ten of her dollars back.

From his sick bed T. Bone shouted: "Hey, what the hell's going on there?"

Duck grunted and his spurs rang as he rutted away. Vineta simply bit the inside of her cheek and thought of blueberry pie.

It didn't take even three minutes before Duck fired off his gun and cried like a loon flying over a lake. Vineta pushed him off and said: "You best git."

"I'm coming back for ye, gal," Duck said, fumbling with his trousers.

"Onliest way I'd be going with you," she said, "is if I was dead and you brought the coffin."

Duck laughed uproariously. All the way up the street.

Chapter Twenty-Seven

John Henry Cole said: "You can't go, Charley. You're not even able to walk without those sticks."

"I can sit and hold a gun," Charley said.

"Hell if you can't, but I doubt there'll be much sitting going on."

Charley knew what Cole was trying to do, get him to acquiesce to Franzetta's will. He appreciated it, but that didn't mean he had to like it. "When you going?" he asked.

"Tomorrow, so we can be in town waiting for them when they come."

"Gonna just face them down in the streets?"

"If that's the way it plays out."

Charley looked at Tom and Preacher Man. "Three of you won't be enough," he said. "I don't suspect Sam Starr is foolish enough to come light."

"Three will have to do," Cole said.

"You think Lou Ford will pitch in? The others?"

"I doubt it."

"I don't know why, then, you're worried about saving their hides."

"It's our mess. We need to clean it up."

Tom said: "You-all do a lot of talking. Seems to me a simple matter. Either go or don't go, either fight or don't fight."

"You think like your mother," Cole said.

"I'd as soon you leave off talking about her," Tom replied.

"Only meant to say she was a black and white woman when it came to decision-making."

"I can see that she was," Tom said, meaning as he said it about her decision to be with Cole in the first place and become pregnant by him. He couldn't figure it out and maybe that was why he'd stayed around, to find out about this John Henry Cole, his father.

"You walk a thin line, Son," Cole warned over this last remark, for he caught the meaning in Tom's words. "I will only allow you so much leeway with me. I don't insult other men and I won't be insulted, even by you."

Both of them knew instinctively, if not by example, that there comes a time in every son's life when he must challenge his father. They each knew, too, that the time was very near at hand.

Preacher Man intervened and said: "We'll need every man if we are to smite our enemies left and right."

"Just need the jawbone of an ass, ain't that right, Preacher?" Charley said.

"I daresay we'll more likely need the blessing of the Almighty and Samuel Colt, considering there is just three of us."

"I dare say," Charley half mocked.

The wind had shifted up from the south and shivered through the trees with an unusual spate of warmth that belied the season. Night had blackened the land and the mood in their hearts. Lou Ford's message was a dark and tragic warning. Every man understands he's bound to die, but it was a different matter to know when that day would come and how it would happen. And for each of them, Charley excluded, it seemed like some sort of indecipherable truth.

Cole, perhaps more than the others, knew with certainty that they could not win, that they could not defeat Sam Starr and his gang, accepting the possibility that Charley mentioned about

Sam Starr's not coming light—that he'd most likely expand his gang for this one mission. Even in their darkest hour as children, Cole could not imagine that his half-brother would have so much hatred toward him as to want to murder him. And even now as Cole looked out the window at the blackness, his heart was absent of that same sort of anger toward Sam, although he would kill him if left no other choice. Cole felt badly that it had come to this, but it was Sam's doing and none of his own.

The worst of it for Cole was the growing sickness when thinking of Tom's dying. The boy should have a chance to live, to marry and have a brood of children and grow old, and not die in a murderous gunfight, because of the violence of men. Nobody should ever die a violent death. It ate and ate at him and he would try again to talk Tom out of going with him. Cole said: "I'm going outside for a smoke. Tom, I'd like to speak to you."

Tom followed his father out and they stood in the darkness while Cole fashioned a shuck and lit it.

"You aim to talk me out of going, don't you?" Tom said.

"You're as good at reading my thoughts as your mother was."

"What'd she see in you to let what happened happen?"

"I don't know," Cole said. "I asked myself that same question a hundred times."

"If she really loved you, why didn't she go off with you?"

Cole exhaled a stream of smoke. "Her father wouldn't let her. He didn't want her marrying a white man, and maybe especially a lawman. I knew how it was, so I just rode out, back to Fort Smith. When I did it, I didn't know she was pregnant, and she didn't, either. I figure she should have told you all that, if she had wanted you to know. But I'm telling it to you now, because I think you should know. When you were born, her father took you away from her, and put you with the folks who raised you. We'd never have met if it weren't that you were with the Caddo Pierce gang, and I was asked to stop the raping and murdering. I know you didn't join in, but you were with them, and that's why you're still in trouble with the law. Let me tell you Anna, your mother, was a righteous woman, and a good person. The second time I left her, and left you with her, I wanted to stay with her more than you will ever know. Anna didn't want it that way. So I did what she wanted."

"A good person . . . the hell she was, if she let you get her pregnant."

Cole's punch was swift, sudden, and it caught Tom on the chin and sent him stumbling. "I warned you not to push it."

Tom came back with a charge, head down, arms windmilling, and caught Cole along the side of his head and momentarily stunned him. Cole grabbed the boy, and they wrestled to the ground, both of them trying to get in blows and both of them succeeding and both of them failing. Tom was strong as a young bear, and it was all Cole could do to hold him down until he weakened from the exertion. Cole was winded, too, and finally stood away and warned: "Let it be."

Tom was on hands and knees, breathing hard.

"I loved her, god damn it, that's all you need to know," Cole said.

"I loved her, too."

And like that, the challenge of son against father was over, the pent up anger of the boy dissipated, at least for the time.

Cole offered him a hand up, but he refused to take it. "I don't want you going with us tomorrow, plain and simple as that."

"I reckon you don't have any damn' say in it, where I go or what I do."

"I'll whip you again, if I have to."

"Hell, you didn't whip me this time, old man." Tom slapped his hat back into shape against his leg.

"You're right, I didn't. And I'm sorry I hit you, and if you want a clean shot at me to get us even, go ahead and take it."

Tom stood there for a moment deciding, then said: "No, I don't reckon I need to whip you any more tonight."

"I don't reckon."

The tension had eased.

Just then Preacher Man came out of the house and saw the two of them standing there, trying still to catch their breaths. " 'Evening, gents," he said, and trudged off to the privy.

Cole left Tom standing there as much to avoid any sense of embarrassment the boy might hold as to get himself a cup of Franzetta's coffee. Charley was sitting at the table, but Franzetta had gone off to their bed. Charley looked up and saw the red mark one of Tom's fists had left on the side of Cole's face, but he didn't comment on it as Cole poured himself a cup of Arbuckle's and sat down across from Charley.

"Jesus, ain't neither one of us fifty years old yet, John Henry, but somehow I feel a hundred. Still, it seems too soon to cash in."

"We all got to go sometime, Charley."

"I told Franzetta I want to go with you tomorrow.

Cole shook his head. "I'm going to have enough on my hands trying to keep an eye on my son, Charley. I don't need to be worrying about you, too."

"You'll not need to worry about me."

"I know I don't, but I will."

"Damn it to hell, John Henry."

Outside, Old Pablo appeared out of the gloaming as he rode up and he saw Tom standing outside, and looked toward the house. "Your *padre* inside?"

Tom nodded.

"Watch my horse, eh, so he don't run off?"

"Sure, why the hell not."

Old Pablo entered the house and saw Cole and Charley, sitting there.

"I smelled the food on the night wind," Old Pablo said.

"What you smelled wasn't no food," Charley said, his dander up because he suspected Old Pablo had come to steal Franzetta. "How many women have you kidnapped in your life and rode off with?"

Old Pablo showed a row of blunt brown teeth. "Plenty."

"Well, I'd kill for her, just so you know."

"*Sí.* I would as well, was she my woman."

"Might still be a biscuit or two left over in the warmer," Cole said.

"Maybe I come for another reason, eh?"

"What would that be, you old reprobate?" Charley asked.

"Look," Pablo said, and opened his long coat. He was wearing three pistols, two about his waist in a gun belt and one across his chest in a holster.

"You look like you're dressed for a dance with the grim reaper," Cole said.

"I am not afraid of death. I welcome it. There is only one thing that I am afraid of . . . rivers. And now with all these guns, if I were to fall into a river, I would surely drown from the weight of them. We're not going to cross any rivers, are we?"

"None I know of," Cole said.

"That's good."

"How'd you know we'd be going?"

"I know what I know," is all Old Pablo said, remaining enigmatic. "I come to fight with you, John Henry. I come to be a brave *hombre* once more. God has whispered in my ear . . . 'Go out like a man, Pablo, not like some old woman, eh?' "

Charley said to Cole: "Well, that ought to make you feel bulletproof, having him along."

"He'll do," Cole said.

"These are good biscuits," Old Pablo said, having reached into the warmer, taken one out, and bit into it.

"And get that filthy old mind off my woman," Charley added.

Old Pablo cackled like a laying hen. "Sure, sure, I'm thinking about a horse I once owned."

"Damned old fool," Charley said. He stood. "Well, I'm off to bed."

They watched him hobble off on his crutches. Fire crackled in the woodstove, and they sat around the table not saying too much, because there wasn't too much to say. Finally Cole said: "We'd best turn in so's to get an early start in the morning."

Cole and Tom, Preacher Man and Old Pablo lay upon pallets around the stove like old dogs, the wood spitting and popping the sap that lay within it like marrow in bone. It was a restless bunch that tried to sleep that night, for there was no comfort in knowing what the next forty-eight hours was likely to bring. Cole had seen so many sweet-faced boys like Tom killed in the war and so many other sweet-faced boys drained of their youth, and still so many more aged beyond their years. He'd often wondered, when he saw them laying in fields or along a stone fence, their hands knotted into fists, their mouths unhinged, their eyes staring into the void, what it must be like for them to cross that final threshold from life to death, either suddenly or slowly. Had they had time to think before they drew their last breath, to mourn the passing from this world without having loved a woman or raised a child of their own? Did everything just end in eternal blackness, or were their spirits rushed to the light he'd heard some claim, the brilliant light of Jesus awaiting them, of Jesus Who took these boys into His loving embrace. Was his other child before Tom showed up—and his only wife, Zee—up there in that glorious heavenly kingdom, too, waiting for him? He hoped, but truly and honestly doubted that it was so. Ask him why he could not fully believe and he would not be able to tell you. He did not know and doubted that he ever would know until that day of his passing arrived. He prayed that he would not have to see Tom thus—hands knotted into fists, eyes staring into the void, jaw unhinged.

CHAPTER TWENTY-EIGHT

Lou Ford did not realize when he left John Henry Cole's place that he'd taken the road to Lusk and not the one to Red Pony. The lateness of the hour, his weariness from a two-day ride, and the blackness of night contributed to his mistake. What was worse, he fell asleep in the saddle and fell off his horse and hit his head and gashed it open.

He wished then and there that he'd never heard of Red Pony, had never taken the job as town marshal. He sat on the ground, holding his head. It throbbed like a rotten tooth. He took off his bandanna and tied it around his skull and couldn't put his hat back on because he had a knot the size of a goose egg. It was cold and he shivered, and he looked about for something with which to make a fire and found a few dry cow flops and got them going well enough to warm himself, though burning cow flops smelled bad.

He figured he might just as well bed down right where he was and make his start for home on the morrow. The cow-flop fire and its warmth and the knock on the head made him sleepy and soon enough he was dreaming of Katy. She seemed as real to him as anything in his waking life. She was warning him about something but he couldn't make out what she was saying. *What?* he thought he said in the dream. *What?*

"I said get yourself up and closer to that fire so I can have a look at you," a man's reedy voice said.

Suddenly Lou knew he had a pistol barrel pressed against his head and it caused the pain to leap in him like a hot piece of lightning. The man's breath was stout with liquor and his words were slurred. A drunken man with a loaded and cocked gun was about the most dangerous thing a fellow could encounter. Lou crawled over closer to the fire.

"Shit," the man said when he saw that Lou Ford was a man of middle age. "You ain't him."

"Ain't who?" Lou Ford said.

"This kid I'm looking for . . . Tom something or other."

Without realizing the consequences Lou blurted out: "Tom Cole, you mean?"

"Yeah, that's it, that's the kid's name. You know him?"

"No," Lou said, realizing his mistake.

"The hell you don't. Why else would you say his name?"

"I was thinking of somebody else."

"Well, unless there is two Tom Coles in this country . . . which I seriously doubt . . . you're a lying son-of-a-bitch and I ought to blow out your brains. Looks to me like they've been blowed out anyway, all that blood soaking through that rag."

Lou swallowed hard. Was this the way the end was going to come? Out here in the great darkness where nobody would even find his body? He thought of Katy as a widow, as maybe marrying another man and living out her days with someone else. He thought of the heartbreak it would bring her to learn of his death. He concluded he would do whatever this fellow wanted of him.

"Yes, you're right," he told the fellow with the gun.

"You're god-damned right I'm right," he said. "Nobody pulls the wool over Duck Leslie's eyes. So, here's the deal . . . you're going to take me to where that son-of-a-bitch lives and we're going there tonight, or else I'm going to leave you a corpse."

Lou Ford nodded, hoping that the drunken man didn't accidentally pull the trigger.

"You packing a pistol?" Duck said, then answered his own question. "Of course you are. Take it out and hand it to me."

Lou did as he was told.

"Well, that's a real pretty little popgun," Duck said, slipping it into his pocket. "Now hand over your wallet, watch, and that ring on your finger."

It was Lou's wedding ring and he hadn't taken it off in years. "Listen, mister, I'd as soon you don't take my wedding band. It means a lot to me."

Duck tapped him on the goose egg and Lou nearly bit his tongue off from the pain. "You think I give two shits about any of that. Take it off!"

Lou took it off and added his wallet just as the fire's flames glinted off Lou's badge.

"Well, what the hell do we have here?" Duck said, ripping the badge from the inside of Lou's lapel. "A damn' lawdog. Ain't this sweet."

Lou said nothing. He knew he was at the mercy of not just a killer but a drunken killer.

"Mount up," Duck ordered, and Lou mounted up. "Now lead out, lovey."

The night never seemed so dark or cruel as it did on the ride back to John Henry Cole's. Lou could hear the man swilling whiskey as Duck rode behind him.

"Don't try and make a run for it. I'll shoot you in the spine." Duck was thinking of T. Bone Blue.

Lou Ford wished he wasn't such a weakling and coward. He wished he had his gun so he could at least shoot it out with this fellow. He wished a lot of things on that ride.

When they came in sight of Cole's place, Lou reined to a halt.

"There it stands, yonder," he said, pointing at the cabin. It wouldn't have been seen at all except for a lamp's glow in one window where Charley had gotten up to squat over the chamber pot, being afraid he'd miss it altogether if he didn't light a lamp.

"You sure this is the place?" Duck said.

"I'm sure. I was out here not but two hours ago."

"And the kid's inside?"

Lou Ford nodded.

Fueled by liquor and greed for that as yet uncollected blood money, and not quite sure of his next move, for men like Duck Leslie hardly ever thought two jumps ahead, he rode up close to Lou and shot him in the back of the head.

Lou's body buckled and then flopped off the horse, dead.

"So long, lawdog," Duck said, feeling pleased with himself.

It had been a mistake on Duck's part, only by then he didn't care. What was killing a kid? Why not let the kid know he was coming. He failed to remember what R.T. had told Vineta about the other fellow. Or maybe it was that Vineta hadn't told T. Bone everything. Hell if it even mattered. Duck finished off the last of his bottle and dropped it beside Lou Ford's body.

John Henry Cole had heard the shot and came instantly alert, reaching for his pistols, expecting it had to do with the Sam and his gang, that they were coming. But then he wondered why would they give a warning shot? It made no sense.

The others remained asleep, including Tom. *Just as well,* Cole thought, *till I can figure out what's happening out there.*

He slipped out the door, a pistol in each hand, cocked and ready to go. He kneeled on one knee, watching until he saw a shadow of movement and against the skyline made out that it was rider, walking his horse up to the cabin slowly. He waited until the rider was close and dismounted, watched as the rider jerked his Winchester from its scabbard and turned toward the front door.

Cole stood up and said: "State your business, mister?"

Duck nearly jumped out of his boots, levered a shell, and

that's when Cole shot him once, then twice, before the man could pull the trigger. Duck did a dance sideways like he'd been staggered by the punches of a prize fighter. Cole moved forward as Duck danced backward, still clutching the rifle. Cole shot him again, and this time Duck fell, the rifle spilling from his hands.

Inside the cabin Charley tripped on the chamber pot and Preacher Man lit another lamp. Tom leaped up, grabbing his pistol, and Old Pablo did the same. They came running out in their long-handled drawers and stocking feet, guns at the ready.

Duck lay gasping like a fish out of water, his whiskey-soaked brain a mass of confusion. *Could it be? Could it be that some son-of-a-bitch shot Duck Leslie?* The question kept repeating itself as he felt his limbs growing colder and colder, as his heartbeat became slower and slower. *Could it be? Could it be?*

Cole stepped forward, his pistol pointed downward at Duck. "What'd you come here for?" he asked.

"Two . . . hundred . . . god . . . damn' . . . dollars," Duck said in gasps.

"To kill my boy?"

"I don't know . . . who's boy he . . . is. . . ."

"Mine, you son-of-a-bitch." And Cole was set to shoot again as much to put the man out of his misery as for revenge, only he didn't have to. Duck took a sucking breath, then quit breathing altogether.

Tom looked on, less certain of himself now that he knew an assassin had come to kill him, now that he realized how fragile and tentative life could be.

Old Pablo stepped forward with one of the lamps in his hand and held it close to the now peaceful repose of Duck Leslie and said: "I know heem. He's the storyteller, always with this Wild Beel, how they do things together, how Beel is killed, hees best frien'. Hees name is Duck something. You believe that? A man, hees name is Duck?"

"Let's carry him into the tool shed for now and bury him in the morning," Cole said. "It's late, and I'm tired."

And so they did.

At first light Tom and Preacher Man and Cole took turns digging a shallow grave a few hundred yards from the cabin, before putting Duck Leslie in his final resting place. Preacher Man prayed over the grave, as he and the others battered by the wind that sought the hilltops and the deepest coulées.

"I declare to you, brothers, that flesh and blood cannot inherit the kingdom of God, nor does the perishable inherit the imperishable. Listen, I'll tell you a mystery. We will not all sleep, but we will all be changed. Death, where is thy victory? Where is thy sting? Amen.

Old Pablo thought it too good a prayer for an assassin.

Breakfast was eaten without appetite or conversation. Charley had agreed to stay behind with Franzetta, even before the killing of Duck Leslie.

"I stay only because I love you too much to go," he'd told Franzetta.

"You are a dear, sweet man," she'd whispered. And though her true longing was for John Henry, she knew that she could live a long, if less than passionate life with Charley. She knew, as every woman knows, that to pretend is not hard. That what *is* hard is to find a man to match her own passion, a man who by his very presence takes her breath away. Charley was not such a man, but John Henry was. But Charley was available to her and John Henry was not. And a good man like Charley was better than no man at all. She was well pleased, she told herself, that Charley was staying behind. She would learn to love him enough.

Cole said: "Charley, the deed to this place is in that trunk at the foot of the bed. Consider it yours."

"I won't," Charley said. "You're coming back."

Cole said nothing in reply. Instead, as soon as they sopped up the last of the milk gravy from their plates, he said: "Let's go. We've got a two-day ride ahead of us that we have to make in one.

They gathered their extra guns and put them in the wagon bed and said their good byes to Charley and Franzetta, figuring it would be their last.

Cole and Preacher Man mounted the wagon seat, while Tom and Old Pablo forked their horses.

Cole suggested they could tie their mounts to the back and ride in the wagon, but Old Pablo protested: "What sort of *hombre* rides in a wagon to go to a gunfight, eh?" The wind nearly snatched away his sombrero, and he had to tighten the stampede string under his chin. "Let us *vaya*," he said.

Charley and Franzetta watched them go.

"I guess that's it, then," Charley said.

Franzetta had nothing to reply. Her stomach was churning with fear that she would never see John Henry Cole again, that Tom would be killed as well, along with the strange Preacher Man. "Do you want more coffee?" she said to Charley.

"I think I do," he said.

CHAPTER TWENTY-NINE

The body of Lou Ford lay on the ground along the road not far from the house. His horse had wandered off into the sedge.

"That's what that shot was," Cole said.

They loaded Lou Ford into the bed of the wagon and covered him with an old blanket Preacher Man had. Next to Lou were the rifles and extra pistols and ammunition in boxes.

"We'll take him home to his Katy," Cole said.

"Hell of a way to start the day," Tom said. "Murder all around."

"I wished you'd go back," Cole said to his son. "Let us handle this mess."

Old Pablo seemed as immune to the death and sudden violence as he was to the cold wind or summer sun. In his native land—that far place to the south—the people even celebrated death during *Día De Los Muertos*. In fact, the cold weather reminded him of this event, for it was held each year on the first days of November—the first day for the children and second day for the adults.

Pablo himself had attended several of these, beginning with the death of his mother, and then a few years later his brother and two cousins. He liked the bright colors, the *musica*, the decorations of orange marigolds and handmade crosses. Trinkets and tequila were offered to the departed, and sugar skulls were consumed. It was a grand time, a time of celebration and remembrance. As far as Pablo knew, the white people had no such ceremony and went about gloomy and long-faced all the time, as though life had been stolen from them and not from the dead. *Come, let us go forth and kill some bad* hombres, he thought, *and God will approve our handiwork, and bless us one and all. Maybe I'll get to heaven yet.*

They rattled along in the wagon, Cole and Preacher Man, while Tom and Old Pablo rode along beside like a rag-tag platoon of men going into a battle and surely defeated before they got there. The wind chased at their backs, and they drew up the collars of their coats. The cold and wind seemed to shrink them. The winter sun was a disk of light that shone dully behind a sky of gauze. The country could be as mean as any man if caught out in it and unprepared. But none of that mattered now as they rode to Red Pony. All that mattered was what awaited them, once they arrived.

A kid of ten or twelve years old, out searching for one of his pa's lost cows, saw them pass along the road, and stopped and watched. He thought he'd never seen anything like it—a parade of *pistoleros*—and the sight of them excited him. He often dreamed at night, when he read dime novels, of becoming a gunfighter, a brave man who saved damsels in distress, of taking on an entire gang of bad men or wild Indians. The fellows passing up the road seemed to him the worst sort of killers, or maybe they were the good guys. He wondered where they were going and what they were going for. He wished he could have ran out and asked to go along.

They rode all day at a steady pace, and then all night. They arrived the very next morning. Cole had loved the town once, but no longer. It was, it seemed to him now as they arrived, that it had become his Valhalla. He glanced once at Tom. *Lord God in heaven, if You exist and if You are compassionate, then let my boy live through this however You may. I thank you.* Cole wasn't used to saying prayers, either on his own behalf or that of others. *I wish I'd got to know him better, that's all I know to say.*

Townsfolk saw them coming and were relieved at the sight of them, knowing that if they came, then the Sam Starr gang might not burn their town, as word had spread among them that this might happen. The word had fallen from the telegrapher's mouth onto their ears, just as Lou Ford expected it would. But Lou Ford no longer had to worry about matters of the living.

They rode straight to Lou Ford's little clapboard house and stopped. Cole climbed down from the wagon and went and knocked on her door. Katy answered it, a comely woman with bright, expectant eyes.

"Katy," Cole said.

She looked past him toward the riders—Tom and Old Pablo, and toward Preacher Man, and did not see her husband among them. He had not returned the night before and she had suspected that he would layover at Cole's place, where he'd said he was headed. But now she did not see him and fear rushed through her like the coldest wind.

"Where's Lou?" she said, her voice breaking.

"He's gone, Katy," Cole said with soft deference. "We brought him to you. He's in the wagon."

Her dignified beauty crumbled, her bright, expectant eyes filled and glistened with tears. "No!" she said. "No!"

Cole took hold of her when she started to collapse. Then she howled like a creature whose leg was trapped, and nearby towns-folk heard her howls and shrank back, believing that it was the first clarion of coming tragedy, that Lou Ford was its first victim, but most likely not its last.

In houses, women began to hide their children much as they would jewels and heirlooms. Men began to contemplate guns for self-defense, to count bullets on a dining room table. Others grew curious and came up the street like a parade of gawkers to see the remains of their marshal, Lou Ford, the last lawman left in Red Pony. They closed in around the wagon, Preacher Man sitting high above them, the reins threaded through his fingers, worried that so many pushing people might spook the mules, so he spoke to them in parables to keep them calm—the mules, not the people.

Tom considered the gawkers more craven than curious, and Old Pablo felt the rush of hot blood through his veins for he had done little since leaving the cabin but think of the men he would help to murder, and, oddly enough, he hoped to be murdered himself so as to be free of the misery of old age and aching bones, of waking slowly each morning, of being woman-less and eating his meals alone, of having to scavenge for what little food there was. He was far, far from his homeland, and, even if he wanted to, he could never return because of all the crimes he'd committed. They would hang him and let the crows have at his eyes. So here he was in the last light of his years, his eyes clouded and full of brown spots, his liver and heart and lungs worn out, his hands freckled with age spots. It was time to go, but not quietly in a bed. Yes, he would die honorably, more honorably than he had lived, and what better could be said of a man than that? *Let them come and kill me and let me kill some of them and I will be happy,* he thought as he eyed the grow-ing crowd of onlookers.

Soon enough Lou Ford's body was carried inside and placed upon the kitchen table, cleared of its dishes and silverware that Katy had set a place for dinner the evening before, expecting that Lou would return and be famished from his ride. *Poor Lou,* she'd thought. *Afterward I will fill him a bath.* They had an old claw-foot cast-iron tub Lou had ordered from the catalogue for Katy, knowing how much she liked her baths. It had taken three men to work it through the narrow doorway and into the house. That first night of its arrival they had heated pails and pails of water and eventually had filled it, and both had undressed and gotten in and sat face to face. Katy had put in bath salts and something to make bubbles, and teased Lou with her lovely little feet and toes. She'd hoped that they could do that again last night. But when he didn't come home, she was disappointed.

Lou lay stiff and bloodless, his skin marbled to an awful gray, his lips a hideous blue. When Katy kissed him, Cole and Preacher Man took their leave and went outside and got aboard the wagon. Cole said to the gathered townspeople: "Every one of you better clear the streets unless you want to join the fight. We'll take every man jack of you. You all know me, and you know that Sam Starr is coming with his gang. We're either going to kill them or they're going to kill us. Either way, there will be bullets flying."

Then he told Preacher Man to drive up the street to the train depot. "We'll meet them there, when they get off the train," Cole confided. "We'll give then a chance to surrender." Cole still figured there was the slimmest of chance that Sam would give it up, instead of them killing each other.

Old Pablo listened with interest to this and smiled wryly. "I don't believe that such men will come here so that you can put them in the calaboose, John Henry."

"I don't believe so, either," Cole said. "But you never know what a man might do until it gets right down to it."

Preacher Man parked his wagon in the back of the depot. "What about other passengers on that train?" he asked.

"That will be the problem," Cole conceded. "We'll have to wait until we can cut them out of the passengers before we try and arrest them."

"And if we can't?" Tom said.

"They'll stick together, no matter what," Cole said. "We've just got to wait until they're clear of any innocents."

"Could be real tricky," Preacher Man said.

"They only know me on sight," Cole said. "Tell you what, Preacher Man, why don't you just wait here, like a man waiting on a train? Old Pablo, why don't you wait over there at the livery, as if you're getting your horse shod? Tom, you wait with Preacher Man."

"Where you going to wait?" Tom said.

"Just up the street there at Grimes's boot shop," Cole replied. "In the doorway. If we get them separated from townsfolk, we'll have them in a crossfire." Cole looked at each one of them. They looked ready. "You watch me, and if I strike a match to light my shuck, you'll know it's them. But you hold your fire until I take the first shot."

They'd armed themselves with extra revolvers and each grabbed a Winchester. They put extra shells in their coat pockets. Old Pablo chose the smallish coach gun instead—a ten-gauge, figuring his eyesight wasn't so good. He wouldn't have to take dead aim, just lift it and pull the triggers. Then they took up their positions, and waited.

Cole waited in the doorway of the boot maker, fashioned himself a cigarette, and left it unlit, surprised at how calm he felt. He thought he might feel anger, or a need for revenge, but he didn't. He simply felt he had a duty to do and he was bound to do it. He didn't want to kill Sam. He just wanted him in prison where he belonged and where, if he stayed long enough, he might be a changed man by the time he got out again. Cole had seen it happen with other men.

He stood mostly hidden from view, his gaze affixed to the depot where Preacher Man and Tom waited on the long bench out front. The long set of railroad tracks shimmered like nickel. The train would announce its arrival before it rounded the last bend. The engineer would pull his whistle chord—a long set of shrieks, letting everyone know it was pulling into Red Pony.

He pictured Sam and the others aboard, armed and ready for

a fight as soon as they stepped from the car, tough men, confident they would succeed in their murder and mayhem. *Not this time,* Cole thought, *not this time.*

From his vantage point, the town looked as though it had been abandoned entirely. Doors had been locked, shades pulled. *Closed* signs hung in the windows. The whole town waited in hiding, and only four armed men stood between them and the coming danger.

CHAPTER THIRTY

Their presence in the railroad car had created an atmosphere of dread—Sam Starr, Shorty Lewis, Black Bill Bryson, Atticus Creed, July and Wordell Cox. Their armament of pistols and rifles, and July's sawed-off shotgun to boot, made a most fearsome presence. But it wasn't just that they were well-armed, it was more than that. They were trail-worn, and dirty with unshaven faces and gunfighter mustaches, shaggy and unkempt. Their hair was long and uncut and greasy. They smelled of horse and sweat and campfire smoke. And their conversation was coarse, without concern for innocent ears.

The porter came by and asked them to watch their tone, and they eyed him hard and said that if he didn't want trouble, he best move on down the line. They bought candy from a candy butcher and licked and sucked it loudly, like oafish schoolboys. They stared at a woman with a bun of auburn hair under a wide hat until she turned around and glared at them, then turned back around and said something to her husband who also turned and looked and withered under their glare.

They took perverse pleasure out of making folks uncomfortable and sauntered back and forth up the aisle and out to the platform where they smoked cigars and talked about the women they'd fornicated with, and when and where, trying to top the others in their lies.

The Cox brothers said whenever they got a woman they shared her and that no woman who lay with them knew one without knowing them both. They passed back and forth a pint bottle of corked bourbon they said they stole off a dead man, and Shorty commented that it was mighty fortunate to come across a dead man who just happened to have a fine bottle of Kentucky bourbon on him. Wordell Cox, the elder of the brothers, chortled and said: "Well, he wasn't exactly dead when we run into him."

July snorted and said: "It was only after he refused to give us his watch and chain he got in that condition."

They had madness lurking in their dark eyes, the sort of madness you might see in the eyes of someone who'd been severely struck in the head with a rock so that it mushed his brain but had not killed the fellow outright.

They undid their flaps and urinated off the platform for sport, reveling in the sight and betting who could send a stream farthest and who could let go longest. They had no shame about exposing themselves. July said to Shorty: "Now you see why we're named the Cox brothers." They laughed at their own joke.

The wind blew some of the stream back and it landed on Shorty's boots, getting them wet. He grimaced and stalked off, and said to Sam Starr: "Those are the craziest bastards I ever run in to."

"Well, it ain't like we plan on marrying them," Sam said. "Once we finish our business in Red Pony, we'll get shed of those boys. I guess, if we was coming to give John Henry Cole a blessing, we'd have hired preachers."

Black Bill among the Starr gang came closest to matching the madness of the Cox brothers. Killing for him was nearly orgiastic. To watch a fellow fold from one of his bullets made him feel god-like. *If there be kings amongst us, then I am one,* he thought. He himself had been shot several times and each time recovered. More than once a medico had said: "I don't know how it's possible that you aren't dead." Bill figured he must be the chosen one, believing at times he was Jesus Christ come again, even though he did not pray or read the Bible or attend any church, although he had burned down a few. Still he believed that he had lived on earth before this time and had come again and that there was a purpose for his existence, though he knew not exactly what that purpose was. Otherwise, why wasn't he dead from all those bullets? Why had he lived when others had died?

He further believed that men were not always who they seemed to be, and because they were not, killing the so-called good ones was actually ridding the world of wolves in sheep's clothing. His late dear sister had often read the Bible to him when they had consorted. And from her readings he remembered such sayings as ". . . wolves in sheep's clothing." His sister Amelia. Fire in the house. Only he and she had escaped. From outside in the cold black night as flames licked the darkness with yellowed tongues, they heard the screams of their parents trapped inside and for a fleeting second they saw their mother's frightened face in the upper window before it exploded into a rain of glass, and then saw her no more.

Left orphans and to their own devices, Bill and Amelia found an old line shack, unused for years, littered with mouse droppings and tangled in cobwebs. Weeds had grown up through the floorboards, but the roof was solid under rain, and Bill had hanged rabbit skins in the two small windows to keep out the wind. They slept on the floor and ate huckleberries and shot rabbits with the gun Bill had grabbed from the burning house—his daddy's sporting gun along with a box of shells.

Luckily it was spring and the weather not so cold and over the summer they settled in, Amelia and him. It wasn't so bad as one might think, as long as there was food for the belly and shelter. Amelia had almost blossomed into a full woman and Bill did not fail to notice it, and soon they were consorting like man and wife, for they had only each other to rely on against the world. Amelia especially seemed to take to her rôle and soon Bill did, too.

She had said: "We are like Adam and Eve in the garden with none to contend with, Bill, but you and me. God would want us to propagate. He would."

Bill had no sense of the meaning of those words but assumed that Amelia did. She was older by one year, and of that same mixed heritage that had never been made fully clear to either of them. But all that blood mixed together had made her beautiful and Bill quite handsome, strong, and tall.

So the nights were awaited with anticipation and the propagating continued apace. It was on one particularly thunderous night that Amelia, now fully mad in her mind, had confessed it was she who'd set the fire, said it with eyes large and wild as a frightened animal's. Care for her body had declined—hair a tangled bush with sticks and grass, hardly ever washed even though there flowed a creek a hundred yards from the shack's front door, her odor offensive even to Bill's nostrils. "I burned them, honey Bill," she had proclaimed. "I burned them up."

"Why?" Bill wanted to know. "Why'd you burn them, Amelia?"

"They was wicked. You just don't know how wicked they was. While you were off a-hunting, they'd do wicked things to me. Oh, Bill, such wickedness did abide in them, I can't even speak its name."

"No." He did not want to believe her about their mam and pap.

"Yes, Bill. They was under the devil's spell. They did such wicked things to me."

She had told how she'd taken a can of coal oil up the stairs that night to the parents' loft and spread it about the bed of the sleepers, then struck a match and touched the flame to the circle of fuel and watched the rope of flame leap up, then scampered out, propping a chair under the door's knob to lock them in. She had then run back down the stairs and rousted Bill from his sleep, shouting: "Fire! Fire!"

The old place was built of dry timber and went up quickly, and then they were gone, those wicked people, much to Amelia's gladness. Whether it was true or not, Bill could not decipher. But he became fearful of Amelia, afraid she might set him afire as well some night, as her madness became all-consuming.

He had strangled her in her sleep. She had struggled only a little. But in the doing—his hands around her thin, fragile throat—her madness, as it left her body, seemed to leap into him like a bolt of lightning. Taking her life had aroused him, as it would often do in future killings, and so he lay with her one last time, speaking tenderly to her as he went, brushing the sticks from her hair, kissing her cool dry mouth.

"Dear sweet child," he had said. "Dear sweet child."

Then in the morning he rose from the connubial bed, and, as she'd done, he burned the shack with her inside it, and walked away. And now, here he was among his own kind, a new family, as it were, men who understood intimately the violence of soul and flesh, who tasted it in their mouths and wore it on their skin and felt it beating in their hearts and flowing in their blood. *If the Almighty didn't want me to be as I am,* he thought, *then why did he make me this way?*

They heard the whistle's shrieks and the conductor announced: "Red Pony, next stop ladies and gents. Red Pony."

The train rounded the last bend and the cars swayed side to side and the motion of them began to slow.

Sam stood up first and said: "You boys get ready."

They stood as well, men strapped to the brim with pistols and cradling rifles and belts with loops filled with cartridges.

"You boys follow my lead when we get off. I'll point out to you John Henry Cole soon as I spot him, if the yellow dog had nerve enough to show up. If not, well. . . ." He offered a strained grin through his grizzled mouth. "We'll think of some way to have some fun."

Shorty and Bill, individually and without the knowledge of the others, had begun to doubt, just a tad, that perhaps this wasn't the wisest move on Sam's part, that it was more personal than business and was the sort of mistake fools made. The train slowed considerably and through the windows they could see the town coming into view. Then came the hard grind of the steel wheels upon the tracks as the engineer applied the brakes, jolting the series of cars behind the engine and causing the gang to stumble a bit and lose their balance some, but they quickly righted themselves and waited for the conductor to set the steps in place so that they could debark.

In moments they'd stepped off the train and stood gathered in a cloud of steam chuffing from the engine that seemed like a great wounded beast as it sat shuddering.

"Which way?" Atticus asked.

Other passengers debarked and flowed around the men like water around rocks.

"I guess follow them till we can find where the marshal's office is and ask him if he delivered my message."

They fell in with the other passengers who were moving in scattered formation toward the heart of town, not knowing that there were guns waiting to knock them down, not believing anyone would stand up against them, the notorious Sam Starr gang.

CHAPTER THIRTY-ONE

"That's them," Tom said when he saw them.

"You sure?" Preacher Man said. "You never seen them before. Are you sure?"

"Yeah, I'm sure," Tom said. "Look how they're dressed, in those long coats. You can see the bulges under there. And look how each of them has rifles. Those fellows are out for blood."

"How can you be sure?"

" 'Cause I used to be a fellow like that a long time ago," Tom admitted.

But the gang members were all mixed in with the other passengers, women and children.

Old Pablo who stood across the street at the livery saw them, too. And just like Tom, an outlaw knows another outlaw when he sees one. The thing he didn't know was which one of those *hombres* was Sam Starr. His gaze affixed to Black Bill because his coloration was much the same as Old Pablo's. He told himself that the dark man was the most dangerous among them and that, when the fight started, he intended to kill that one first.

John Henry Cole saw them from his vantage point in the boot maker's doorway. Sam hadn't changed much, just older and heavier, but he would have recognized his half-brother anywhere. He had the match in his hand, his thumbnail set to strike it and hold it to the shuck that dangled from the corner of his mouth, but there were too many passengers in the way.

He cursed under his breath. If he let them get too far, he couldn't trap them in a crossfire.

He made a quick decision and stepped from the doorway and into the middle of the street and fired his rifle into the air. The sudden gunshot scattered the passengers like a covey of quail, stranding Sam and his boys—Atticus Creed, Black Bill, Shorty, and the Cox Brothers.

"Halt where you are and throw up your hands!" Cole commanded.

They stopped all right, and looked at him as if he was a crazy man, figuring him to be just one against the five of them.

"You dumb son-of-a-bitch, Cole!" Sam shouted. "I din't figure you to commit suicide, but it looks like that's what you gone and done."

There was about forty yards between them.

"Boys," he said, without turning to his companions, "yonder stands before you the famous John Henry Cole, slayer of men."

Old Pablo pulled the coach gun from under his coat and stepped into the street behind the gang.

Tom and Preacher Man stood as one levering their Winchesters.

The commotion caused some of the gang to turn and see the odds were getting about even and that the killing might not be quite so easy as they'd been led to believe.

"You can surrender your arms and allow yourself to be arrested, or you can go the hard way," Cole said. "It makes not a damn' dime's worth of difference to me."

"An old man and a boy and that silly-looking fellow in the paper collar?" Sam said derisively. "Well, hell, let's see how it works out then."

"If that's what you want," Cole said.

The gunfire erupted all at once, everybody shooting at everybody, or so it seemed. Bullets ricocheted and splintered wood and shattered glass and kicked up cold dirt and rended flesh and broke bone. Blood spilled and pain flamed and the world spun and time ceased. The gods of Ancient Greece surely would have enjoyed the show, and had it been a Greek tragedy, surely they would have come up with a plan to lower one of them down in a basket and bring resolution to the conflict, a *deus ex machina.*

Tom shot Wordell Cox, and Wordell shot Tom, both firing at the exact same moment at one another. Wordell's bullet nicked Tom's forearm and cut it open as if he'd swiped it with a razor. Tom's bullet struck the more telling blow, punching Wordell in the guts and spinning him like a cheap child's top.

Old Pablo knocked down Bill with a single blast, just as he'd planned it, and part of Bill's leg disappeared into a bloody spray. But July Cox had taken careful aim and fired two slugs dead center into Old Pablo, and he fell instantly dead as stone.

Bill looked down at his missing leg, the pain flaring both ways up and down. He cursed and wet himself at the same time.

Tom, in spite of his injury, took out Shorty with a round to the back of the head that pitched Shorty face down into the earth. It was the third man Tom had shot in the last few days. And when he saw the explosion of blood and brain and offal that sprayed from Shorty's skull, it caused Tom to wince.

Atticus stood coolest among them and his first shot hit Preacher Man in the groin sending him down. Then he turned and took aim at Tom who saw what was happening and pitched sideways. But Atticus's bullet struck Tom in the hip and put him down.

Sam and John Henry—brothers of a kind—had both fired as one and surprising to both men their bullets missed the mark. Sam Starr ran for cover inside Tanner's Hardware, crashing bodily through the plate glass window. Cole went in pursuit.

July tried pulling his brother Wordell to his feet, but it was no good.

"Let me be!" the brother cried. "It's like a hot spike driven into my guts! Oh, Jesus!" His eyes were wet with tears that had streaked his grimy cheeks and snot leaked from his nostrils and collected in his mustache.

"You got to get up," July commanded.

"I can't, god damn you."

Tom had taken refuge behind a baggage cart loaded with trunks of various types. He laid down such a withering fire that Atticus had a hard time returning a shot.

Son-of-a-bitch is good, Atticus thought. *Too good.*

Preacher Man held himself against the flame of pain eating up his groin. His hands were wet with blood and he couldn't tell if his manhood was gone or not. He tried to crawl away, but even to move a few simple feet was as mighty a task as knee-walking across Egypt. He thought of the carnal sins he'd committed and considered this was God's punishment for his former life. Maybe. Who knew the mind of God? He found himself praying amid the tears of pain, wondered if he was dying. Wondered what heaven would truly look like once he got there. *If* he got there.

Wordell puked all over July's boots.

July cursed.

Cole moved toward the hardware store, a pistol in each hand, knowing they were better than a rifle for close-in work. He realized it was probably suicidal to go in the front way. He figured that Sam would seek the other hole and went instead up an alley and around back, and waited. Sure enough, in less than a minute more, the back door of the hardware swung open, and Cole took aim.

Only it wasn't just Sam who emerged. He had Tanner's wife with him, his arm around her neck, half dragging, half carrying

229

her. She was panicking loudly and he said: "I will blow your god-damn' head off, woman, if you don't stop that caterwauling, you stupid cow!"

Cole thumbed back the hammer of his right-hand revolver, and when he did, it drew Sam Starr's attention, and he swung around, Tanner's wife between them.

"Like I said, you're a stupid son-of-a-bitch, Cole. You always thought you could best me when we was kids. Just because you were bigger and tougher. Well, look who's tougher now."

He fired and suddenly Cole was looking at a dull gray sky. The bullet's impact had stunned him. He heard someone running, someone crying.

When Atticus ran out of rifle shells, he drew one of his several pistols and tried to find a spot to take down Tom behind that baggage cart, but it offered good cover. Atticus called to July to come and help him kill the kid, and July, his anger such he would have killed his own mother, came forth, both guns blazing.

Tom knew he could not survive the assault much longer, both of them firing and closing the gap. He was bleeding and hurting badly and was reloading as fast as he could but was nearly out of bullets. He wanted to take out at least one more of them before he died and so held his fire, waiting for them to come around the cart—it was the only way they could get to him, around the cart.

From where he lay he could see Old Pablo lying dead not a dozen feet away. And he could hear Preacher Man's anguished groans. *I'm next,* he told himself. He thought of his mother in that good place. *I'm coming,* he told her silently. Then suddenly he saw Sam Starr, running out of the end of an alley, a gun in his hand.

"Kill the kid behind the cart!" July Cox shouted. "He's the last one left."

"Damn it to hell," muttered Tom. "Time to go down."

He pushed in the last shell, then stood awkwardly and firing at the same time, levering shells and laying down a spraying fire, fast, fast, fast. But not fast enough because he was hit twice in the span of a blink. It felt just like being busted by a man swinging a shovel blade as hard as he could across your chest. It stole his air for a moment and felt like a boulder had fallen on him. *That's it, then,* he told himself as he lay there, staring upward. And for the longest most beautiful moment of his existence, there was complete silence and Tom closed his eyes peacefully, welcoming death, ready for the ride.

But then more gunshots came and he opened his eyes and turned his head enough to one side to see John Henry Cole, a pistol in each hand, his shirt wet with blood, closing on the trio of killers—Atticus Creed, July Cox, and Sam Starr. Tom saw the father he barely knew, now a killing machine, as he dropped first one man and then the other, even though they had begun to return fire. Cole seemed to walk right through the rain of bullets. Be it luck or blessing granted him from somewhere, no more bullets struck him and he knocked down the men like bowling pins. For the merest moment he and Sam Starr stood only ten feet apart and it almost seemed like they were kids again, playing lawman and outlaw and taking turns dying. Now it was for real. Each man fired and Sam fell dead, a bullet through his brain.

Suddenly it was over. The whole affair had lasted just minutes. The dead were dead and the wounded the wounded. And standing in the street alone was John Henry Cole, his guns empty, bloody and bowed, but still standing when no other did.

He came then to Tom and knelt next to him and said: "Will you live or will you die, young son?"

"I don't know," Tom said.

"I do," Cole said.

Chapter Thirty-Two

In a house far distant from where the battle had taken place, Vineta approached the bed-ridden T. Bone Blue and said: "Let me ask you something."

He was prickly because he had not yet heard back from Duck Leslie. He should have by now, unless the Duck had absconded with the hundred dollars. *Damn his very soul if he has screwed me out of that money,* he had thought just as Vineta had come into the room, ready to pose her question.

"What is it?" he said sourly. "All the time with questions. Can't a woman ever leave a man be?"

"Yes, I can let you be," she said calmly. "But I want to ask you just one thing first."

"Well, go the hell ahead then and ask."

"Did you steal my money?"

"No. What the hell would I steal your money for?"

"You were always the worst liar I ever met, T. Bone Blue."

"So what if I did? Ain't I got a right to some happiness and peace?"

"You stole it and gave it to that ugly bastard, Duck Leslie, didn't you?"

"You seem already to have the answer, why you asking me?"

"Just this," she said, and pulled a Derringer and shot him between the eyes.

"Good night, sweet prince," she said, then shot herself with the other bullet.

As it turned out the wounds suffered by both father and son were not as serious as they seemed, but Preacher Man's was more so. He would be laid up a time in the infirmary—longer than Tom and Cole would be.

The doctor said to Preacher Man: "And of course, your pizzle will be out of action sometime, maybe forever, sorry to have to tell you."

"Well," Preacher Man returned, "it wasn't like I was using it that much anyway. For every time there is a season, and for everything there is a reason."

The doctor said: "That laudanum I gave you seems to have taken hold. Enjoy it, Preacher Man."

Several weeks passed without word from Cole or the others. Charley and Franzetta had given in to the idea that they were all gone forever, that what had been feared had come to pass.

Charley repeated his regret that he hadn't gone along, and Franzetta reminded him of his promise to care for her.

"As soon as I get well enough," Charley said, "I'm riding to Red Pony and learn what happened, and make sure those boys got a decent burial. It's the least I can do."

Charley and Franzetta were out in the yard, Franzetta hanging up the wash and Charley doing his best to split more firewood, when they saw a wagon rattling up the road, pulled by a pair of matched mules. Tied to the back was a ragged old horse with a cheap saddle and Tom's spotted paint.

"Lord, it looks like them," Charley said. "Some of them at least."

"They'll need caring," Franzetta said. Both Cole and Tom still wore bandages.

"We'll care for 'em," Charley said. When the wagon rattled up to where they stood, Charley said: "Welcome home."

ABOUT THE AUTHOR

Bill Brooks is the author of twenty-five novels of historical and frontier fiction. After a lifetime of working a variety of jobs, from shoe salesman to shipyard worker, Brooks entered the health care profession where he was in management for sixteen years before turning to his first love—writing. Once he decided to turn his attention to becoming a published writer, Brooks worked several more odd jobs to sustain himself, including wildlife tour guide in Sedona, Arizona where he lived and became even more enamored with the West of his childhood heroes, Roy Rogers and Gene Autry. Brooks wrote a string of frontier fiction novels, beginning with *The Badmen* (1992) and *Buscadero* (1993), before he attempted something more lyrical and literary in the critically acclaimed: *The Stone Garden: The Epic Life of Billy the Kid* (2002). This was followed in succession by *Pretty Boy: The Epic Life of Pretty Boy Floyd* (2003) and *Bonnie & Clyde: A Love Story* (2005). *The Stone Garden* was named by *Booklist* as one of the top ten Westerns of the decade. After that trio of novels, Brooks was asked to return to frontier fiction by an editor who had moved to a new publisher and he wrote in succession three series for them, beginning with *Law For Hire* (2003), then *Dakota Lawman* (2005), and finishing up with *The Journey of Jim Glass* (2007). *The Messenger* (Five Star, 2009) was Brooks's twenty-second novel. *Blood Storm* (Five Star, 2011) was the first novel in a series of John Henry Cole adventures. It was praised by *Publishers Weekly* as a well-crafted story with an added depth due to its characters. *Booklist* said of *Winter Kill* (Five Star, 2013), the third John Henry Cole story: "Western fans are largely forced to survive on reprints originally published decades ago, which makes the work of contemporary writers like Brooks, who haven't abandoned the grand Western tradition, all the more satisfying." Bill Brooks now lives in northeast Indiana. His next Five Star Western will be another John Henry Cole story titled *Go and Bury Your Dead.*